GENERAL BIPIN RAWAT
The Warrior

GENERAL BIPIN RAWAT
The Warrior

Manjeet Negi

PRABHAT PRAKASHAN

Published by
PRABHAT PRAKASHAN PVT. LTD.
4/19 Asaf Ali Road,
New Delhi-110 002 (INDIA)
e-mail: prabhatbooks@gmail.com

ISBN 978-81-961590-9-2
GENERAL BIPIN RAWAT: The Warrior
by Shri Manjeet Negi

Edition
First, 2023

Translator
Hemendra

Price
₹ 500.00 (Rupees Five Hundred only)

Printed at
R-Tech Offset Printers, Delhi

Preface

General Bipin Rawat was a valiant soldier and a competent strategist. During forty years of his military career, he made significant contributions to the progress of the country and the Indian Army. He was not only popular among soldiers but among the public as well for his simple life, selfless service and decisive leadership. He was very positive in his thinking and was a visionary. He used to think in entirety and take decisions in totality. His deeds reflected his sharp mind and inclusiveness in his actions.

General Bipin Rawat was a great military strategist. He played an important role in conceptualising the surgical strikes across the Myanmar and Pakistan borders. As a COAS (Chief of the Army Staff) and later as the CDS (Chief of Defence Staff), he took a number of admirable and bold actions during the Doklam crisis and anti-terrorism operations in J&K. Creation of an 'Integrated Battle Group' was the outcome of his most ambitious planning. He also worked hard at the structural planning of the integration of Armed Forces, keeping in mind the security needs of the country, but could not witness its implementation during his lifetime.

General Rawat was taking positive steps in the direction of fighting the future wars with indigenous arms and equipment. He had been paying particular attention to cyber, space, electronics, robotic warfare and artificial intelligence.

He had prepared a broad roadmap for modernisation and skill enhancement of the three Forces. His humility and gentle demeanour was acknowledged and respected by even his foreign counterparts.

In short, his splendid personality was a confluence of a valiant soldier, military strategist and sociable person. This book by Manjeet Negi highlights to a great extent his remarkable and unique personality and various shades of his working style. We would always be indebted to General Bipin Rawat's selfless service to the nation and he would forever remain in our memories.

—Ajit Doval
National Security Advisor

Foreword

Leadership is of immense importance to the military profession. Judgement, competence and courage often account for more than the armed might alone in achieving success. 'Generalship' is carefully studied by other leaders who will lead men in combat, whether or not they reach General-officer rank themselves. Over time, the Indian Armed Forces have produced an impressive list of senior officers who have ably demonstrated the importance of leadership in trying circumstances.

An officer and soldier in their military career, seek to be inspired by senior military leadership that leaves an indelible impression on the mind, be it as a dynamic and inspiring personality, a person with strong courage of conviction who always 'walk the talk' or a person who by his very vivaciousness, leaves you seeking his company and looking forward to more. During my long military career, my fortune in meeting the late General Bipin Rawat was exactly this.

General Bipin Rawat and I grew up together in the same regiment. In fact, before I knew General Bipin, I had met his father, Lt Gen Lakshman Singh Rawat, who was GOC (General Officer Commanding) of Maharashtra and Gujarat areas besides being the Colonel of 11 Gorkha Rifles. As a Commander, I had also presented the 'Colonel' with a Guard of Honour at Bakloh in 1985.

The opportunity to work closely with General Bipin Rawat arose when I was appointed as the DGMO (Director General of Military Operations). It was in this appointment that I got insight into his thinking which transcended from tactical to strategic level, his ideas about bringing change in the Army, civil-military relations, domestic politics, inter-service relations, etc.

He also had a good understanding of the operational challenges we face in eastern Ladakh, central sector, Sikkim and Arunachal Pradesh. He advocated building strong capabilities before any deliberate military action.

Owing to his all-round experience, he was first appointed as the Chief of the Army Staff and then subsequently, he went on to become the country's first Chief of Defence Staff. This indeed was a great recognition as he had met all the challenging and diverse requirements in his career with aplomb, foresight and due diligence. He firmly believed that in order to ensure seamless and unbreachable security of our nation, the three Services, viz. Army, Navy and Air Force needed to work in absolute coherence and in an integrated manner. He has left behind an indelible mark, a formidable legacy as well as a long list of unfinished visionary tasks that need to be brought to the desired levels of closure. Despite several hurdles and challenges, General Bipin Rawat had a clear vision and unflinching understanding of how to bring certain transformational reforms to further modernise and bolster the capabilities of the Indian Armed Forces.

In spite of multifarious responsibilities, General Bipin Rawat never neglected the regiment to which he credited his professional growth. On being nominated as the CDS, he decided to hand over the responsibilities connected with the regiment to me. On 12 November, 2018, he came to Lucknow for the Golden Jubilee celebration of the Gorkha Rifles Regimental Centre and there he handed over the command of the 'Colonel of the Regiment' to me. In this ceremony, 150 military officers, 1,500 NCOs and men from India and Nepal were also present. After all, General Bipin Rawat was also an honorary General of the Nepalese Army. After two months of handing over of this command, on 1 January, 2020, the then Chief of Army Staff General Bipin Rawat became the nation's first Chief of the Defence Staff.

One of the biggest achievements of General Bipin Rawat was to bring in the 'change'. He challenged old perceptions, ideas and practices. The change he attempted was for not only keeping the Armed Forces 'ready' to meet operational challenges, but also relevant for meeting larger goals of nation building.

General Bipin Rawat dedicated his entire life to the service of the Armed Forces and the nation. Because of his untimely demise, India lost a great patriot, a brave General and a visionary military strategist who has left behind an enormous void. It will be our earnest endeavour to pursue his visionary dreams of transforming our Armed Forces and contributing further towards nation building.

Manjeet Negi is associated with media and has been a Defence Correspondent for a long time. He has had the good fortune of witnessing the remarkable work of General Bipin Rawat through various stages of his career. He has had long and deep thoughtful conversations with him on multifarious issues related to the development of the Armed Forces and other contemporary issues pertaining to national interest.

This book, authored by Shri Manjeet Negi, is an honest tribute to the sacrifices and contributions of the late General Bipin Rawat and which will remain forever etched in the annals of the history of Indian Armed Forces and our country at large. In my opinion, this book has certainly brought to light many aspects of late General Bipin Rawat's illustrious career that may not be known to many. These exquisite and detailed accounts would surely serve as an inspiration for the readers and the future generations of our country.

—General Anil Chauhan
Chief of Defence Staff

Contents

Author's Pen

It is impossible to portray a character like Bipin Rawat. With such diverse colours and shades to his personality and vastness of his character, any canvas may seem too small, allowing depiction of only a hazy picture.

"Army is not a job. Those who consider it a job, they are advised not to join the Army; they could go anywhere, take any other employment, but not with the Army. Only those who can sacrifice their lives for the country, must come into the Army." The passion of sacrificing one's life for the country was such that for him home, family, relations were secondary.

These words of General Rawat kept resounding in my ears during the whole night of 8 December, 2021. During my 20 years' career as a Defence Correspondent, I had been reporting about the tenures of various Chiefs of three Services. I must truly say that all the Service Chiefs had reached these positions due to their efficiency and abilities, but honestly speaking, General Bipin Rawat was the only Gerneral, who had been working for all the three Services relentlessly and always following the 'nation first' policy, keeping the family, relations and all others after.

Whenever I met General Rawat, he always used to tell me, "*Bhula!* I have to return to Uttarakhand, where I want to start a good boarding school for children." He always said that after retirement, he would open a school in Garhwal and another at Kumaon. These modern boarding schools would be on the pattern of Mayo College. Recently, he had performed the *bhoomi pujan* (worship of house) at Dehradun. The General called me on Sunday, the 5th December to his house in Dehradun and told me that he would soon be going to Uttarakhand after finishing the work of the Theatre Command. How could anybody express in words the intensity of love that this true nationalist, patriot and son of Uttarakhand had for his soil?

I, as a journalist, had an opportunity to closely watch his modus operandi, from his becoming COAS in 2016, till his death as the CDS in 2021. Whenever he was in Delhi, I would meet him almost daily, sometimes regularly for days together. Gradually I developed a relationship of a younger brother to him rather than that of a journalist. He always called me, *Bhula*, younger brother. He not only called me younger brother, he even treated me with elder brotherly affection.

Whenever I met him, we used to have elaborate discussions on what the Forces could do for the country, what could be their role during peace time and how they can improve their roles for the country and the society. He had a reservoir of plans and schemes for the Services, military personnel and for their welfare. He devoted each and every moment during his tenure as COAS to CDS, for the modernisation of all the three Services. He truly liberated the Indian Army from the British Army traditions and transformed it into real Indian Army. The inconsistencies and traditions, which were prevalent prior to his joining as COAS, were changed.

A person as a correspondent being influenced by a person means that he may not remain unbiased about him. But his imposing persona, his strong character and unparallel skill, his usual simplicity, all were so natural and influential that anybody meeting him more than once, was likely to be greatly impressed by him. His military strategies, work readiness, his studies, analysis, fearless, independent and forthright interpretations, his heroic deeds, humane impartiality and 'zero tolerance' of corruption were capable of converting any neutral and independent person in his favour. But, so far as I was concerned, I was happy that he treated me as his younger brother.

The path for changes has never been easy and smooth. It's in fact a difficult call to change the status quo and that too in a positive direction. He had to face stiff opposition even within the Army, but he ignored it. He was confident that his mission was in national interest and that it was a visionary mission with far-reaching consequences. It was for the betterment of the future of the Indian Armed Forces. Though his mission was full of hazards, he never faltered in his efforts. The reforms he suggested for the Army were first applied on his own self. He followed a zero tolerance policy against violation of ethical values and corruption in the Army. He was the most ardent pioneer of 'Make in India' in the Armed Forces. In spite of internal conflicts between DRDO and the three Forces, he supported production of weapons and military hardware in the country itself. He faced more diverse and challenging responsibilities than any other earlier General could have and completed those successfully. Apparently, these factors must have been considered prior to handing over him the responsibility of the joint command of the three Services. The Modi government took nine months in deciding about the appointment of second CDS, which indicates how intense efforts were entailed in selecting a suitable substitute for CDS Rawat.

But, I have written this book as an unbiased writer. Not only certain controversial things and issues about him, but the perspectives have also been included in the book, through which I have considered all these facts. Nevertheless, I am of the opinion that it is very difficult to wrap up the personality of CDS Bipin Rawat and his work in such a small book and it is almost impossible for a writer like me to do justice to each and every shade of his grand character. I leave it to the readers to judge how far I have been successful in portraying this larger-than-life personality.

I express my sincere thanks for the co-operation extended to me in completing this great tale, to Kritika and Tarini, the two daughters of late General Bipin Rawat and Mrs Madhulika Rawat, Colonel Satyapal Singh Parmar and Brigadier Shivendra Singh. I am also grateful to Shri Ajit Doval, National Security Advisor and General Anil Chauhan, CDS. My wife Chetna Negi deserves special mention for her continuous support in all my endeavours. I am grateful to Mayank Singh for going through the entire manuscript and finalising it. I sincerely thank Yogamber Singh Bisht for his co-operation.

I salute the first CDS, the great warrior, Bipin Rawat. My heart-felt tribute to the General!

—Manjeet Negi

1

Larger than Life

From Delhi to Devbhumi

General Bipin Rawat lived a 'larger than life' life, which may not be possible for many others in their normal lifetime. His life is like a lighthouse of inspiration to live.

Every land has its own character. Somewhere it is fertile for wheat, whereas at other places, rice or spices grow in abundance. A land produces hockey players, whereas another is the mother of wrestlers or boxers. The land of Uttarakhand has been producing bravehearts and is still giving birth to warriors. This land has been the 'mother of braves'. It would be impertinent to list such bravehearts and moreover, such a list would be unending. Here, generations of martyrs, warriors and brave soldiers have been rendering excellent service to the Army and this is an endless process, which continues incessantly. It is impossible and illogical to compare the brave sons of the land with each other. But, we can say that General Bipin Rawat was the first brave son of this land to reach the topmost post of CDS. Following family tradition, he was destined to join Army. Since childhood, he was determined to serve in the Army, but none has ever succeeded in reaching those heights that he had set for himself. It may be mentioned that there are families whose members of second or third generation have provided their services to the Army as officers, but General Bipin Rawat was the first person, probably of fourth generation of his family, to have served the Army. This son of a former Vice Chief of the Army, not only served the Indian Army, but also had the privilege to lead the combined strength of Indian Air Force and Indian Navy. Undoubtedly, General Bipin Rawat's saga of glory is highly motivational.

Deeprooted

It was Monday, 30 April, 2018, when the festival of Budh Purnima was being celebrated. But the festivities and elation in this tiny hilly village of Saina, under the Birmoli village *panchayat* of Dwarikhal Block of Uttarakhand's Pauri district, had a different meaning. Today, one of their nearest ones was coming to the village from far off and the village was filled with pride at this visit. Bipin Rawat of their village had assumed the charge of COAS on 1 January, 2017 and subsequently he was visiting his village for the first time. Bipin Rawat's village is known for the fact that at least one member of each family of the village serves the Indian Army. As such, the significance of the visit of the Army Chief for the villagers is easy to understand. Though it was Chief of the Indian Army who was visiting the village, but he was uncle for some, brother for others and father-in-law or linked with other relations with the villagers of Saina. For this visit of Saina, General Bipin Rawat was no less enthusiastic than the people of the village.

Had he so desired, he could have landed by a helicopter in his village, but he decided to leave the Army helicopter at the Garhwal Rifles Regimental Centre, Lansdowne and chose to head for his village by road. He wanted to see and feel the hilly roads to his village. Saina is a small village of just a few houses. Due to migration of people to cities for education and jobs, the village families had been left with very few children, adolescents and youth. The village is meagerly populated at present; there are a few retired persons, elderly people, unemployed youth and women left behind. Being a village which was located in a difficut area and was cut off from road connectivity, it was deprived of witnessing township development. There is no motorable *pucca* road leading to this village. As such, the sixty-year-old COAS had to cross the rugged hilly track on foot. The General trekked this steep track of more than a kilometre in length on foot and at a very fast speed.

Father Lt Gen Lakshman Singh and mother Sushila Devi of General Bipin Rawat

General Bipin Rawat was not born in Saina village. His birth took place in Dehradun and he could not spent much of his early times there. So far as the Rawat title is concerned, it is customary for the Rajputs of Uttarakhand to use this title with their names. It is a military title or a military decoration, which was allowed by the rulers of Garhwal to Rajputs, who were experts in military tactics and were great warriors. When it came to Saina, General Bipin Rawat had great attachment and love with the village and people and that is why he considered it his native village. His forefathers belonged to this village. In view of his roots and love for the soil of this land, one can easily measure his passion and devotion to not just Saina, but the entire country.

With his relatives in Saina village, after becoming Army Chief

His father had shifted to Dehradun for education of his children. Thus, before they shifted to Dehradun, he had a good time in Saina which has members of his blood relations still staying there. Even today, after retirement from the post of Hawaldar in the Army, his uncle Bharat Singh Yadav's family, his other uncles, aunt, etc. are still residing in the village. Even after reaching the topmost post in the Army, he was deeply rooted to his native place. Love for Uttarakhand, the birthplace of his ancestors, often could be felt in his talks. The hill culture was engrained in him. As such, whenever General Rawat got any opportunity in his tight busy schedule, he would visit this place. This time too, on his visit to the village, he went to pay his obeisance to his family deity, Gool. He met all the villagers and his relatives with love and warmth, got snapped with the entire family and expressed concern over the deserted village due to migration. He stayed in the village for more time than expected.

Not only the Saina village, he also visited his maternal grandfather's village, Dhanari along with his wife on 20 September, 2019. He had visited this village during his childhood many times. This Dhanari village in Uttarkashi district is the parental house of General Bipin Rawat's mother, Sushila Devi. His mother Sushila Rawat was the daughter of Thakur Surat Singh Parmar, a prominent personality of Uttarkashi. Her younger uncle, Kishan Singh Parmar had been MP and MLA from Uttarkashi. His elder maternal grandfather, Thakur Sahib Singh Parmar was also a well-known person in the area. When Bipin Rawat became the Army Chief, there were Diwali-like celebrations in his maternal grandfather's village. This time also, his maternal uncle and the villagers extended him a traditional warm welcome. General Bipin Rawat also gave presents to his childhood friends and cousins. He enjoyed *puri* and *dal* fritters. Alongwith wife, he went to worship Goddess Pitambari in the temple of Raj Rajeshwari with religious rituals and returned after spending an enjoyable time in his maternal grandfather's village.

Efforts for Development

Bipin Rawat dreamt to build a grand house in Saina, the village of his ancestors, where a number of his relatives had been residing. He wanted to do substantial social work in Saina and in the maternal/parental village, Dhanari. He wished to build good roads and a hospital in his village, after his retirement. He had told the villagers and his other acquaintances about his desire to live mostly in the hills after retirement. Bipin Rawat had also started the construction of his house amidst the forest in the picturesque valley of Premnagar in Dehradun. His wife Madhulika was also very happy with this decision of his.

Bipin Rawat had planned to facilitate the return of the villagers, who had migrated from the village and rehabilitate them in the village. He had promised to work on a project which would not only attract the migrants to return to the village, but would stop their migration for good. He wanted to provide efficient medical facilities to the villagers and to people from nearby villages. He had decided to make sincere efforts in this direction. He was bent on providing facilities and information about enrolment of youth of Pauri district in the Army. This all he had promised to himself.

Family of Braves

Bipin Rawat's mother, born in Dehradun, belonged to Parmar clan of Rajputs, whereas his father was a Chauhan Rajput. Both the Rajputs were known for their military service, bravery and valour. Birth, upbringing and education in such a family were enough in building a person into a valiant braveheart. Trilok Singh, Bipin Rawat's grandfather, had been a Subedar in the Army. He was posted at Lansdowne Cantonment. Father Lakshman Singh Rawat was enlisted as a sepoy or a soldier, but when he retired, he was nearing the top post in the Indian Army. He retired as Lt Gen and had an array of achievements and medals to his credit. One can only imagine the various traits, like courage, martial competence, sustainability, determination and ability that this man possessed. There was an environment of patriotism and military dominance in the family. The family was an epitome of patriotism and devoted to the Army.

Two brothers, Bipin and Vijay, in their childhood

It was natural for Bipin, born to such a brave soldier, to inherit such instincts of valour and dedication to the motherland from the brave family.

Like every father, Lakshman Singh also wanted his son to join the Army and become a higher officer than himself and with this in mind, he arranged for a well-planned education for his son. The beginning was from the Convent of Jesus and Mary, the best school of Dehradun for primary and secondary education, which was co-educational. The purpose of admission to this school was to lay a strong foundation of education and to provide wholesome environment with a sense of gender equality. This was just a beginning. Soon he was admitted to a prominent school of Dehradun—Cambrian Hall School, which was considered to be one of the best school education centres, which again was a co-educational school where he studied for three years. *Khukri* was the symbol of the school and its motto was 'To Greater Heights'. Relation of the *Khukri* symbol with Bipin Rawat's life was long lasting. The symbol of his Gorkha Rifles Regiment, which he joined later, too was the *Khukri*. Inspired by the school motto of 'To Greater Heights', he continued to reach greater heights in life. He visited his Cambrian Hall School on 10 September, 2017, where he had said that he was proud to come true to the motto and symbol of the school.

Education and Morals

Not that father Lakshman Singh Rawat, third generation in Army, alone wanted his son to serve the Army, even the child Bipin Rawat was eager to join the Army. Had Bipin Rawat chosen any other career away from family traditions, it would have been seen as an aberration! Bipin was destined to join Army. His father was a role model for him. Who can be such fortunate to find one's motivation so close? If the ideal is present in the family itself, then thoughts and deeds find a definite direction, which not only makes the road to the destination much easier, but also strengthens the determination and improves the capabilities and skills. After completing his education, he was sent to Saint Edward School in Shimla for further education, from where he was to clear intermediate and leap to educational and professional heights.

A couple of his teachers in intermediate and high school have shared memories of this student's life. The media contacted his school teachers on his reaching new heights to learn whether the events during his student life were casting their shadows on Bipin Rawat's future. A son, who had acquired good manners from a cultured family and discipline from good schools, cannot be expected to get spoiled with the normal vices of the age. However, there is every possibility of a son from an affluent family to be indifferent to education and hard work or turning arrogant, ill-tempered and uncivilised. But a teacher of a high school told, "He was industrious from the beginning and he always tried to finish his work with minimum labour and time, but he did not approve of shortcuts. He was a fearless and frank boy." An intermediate teacher spoke highly of Bipin Rawat saying that he was an intelligent boy from the very beginning and not only scored high marks or performed better in his subjects, he used to surprise us by his 'out of the box thinking'

and 'innovative ideas'. Whenever he borrowed any idea from any source or any individual, he used to give credit for the idea to the concerned person or the source. Of course, he was a polite person, but he used to present his views with determination and boldness. He was not from a civilian background, but he was very social. This was due to the distinguishing trait, which was avoidance of dominance over others with his knowledge, family, rank, etc. General Rawat's bold decisions exhibited that he believed in winning hearts rather than dominance and privileges. I remember he had said while sharing his experiences with school students, "The lessons of humanity that I learnt as a child in the school, could never be forgotten and these became my greatest strength." An eye-witness to his student life says, "Simplicity, elegance, honesty, innovative thinking in every field, made him unique among other students."

Favourite Game—Football

Young Bipin had lesser liking for indoor games; he was fond of laborious field games. Football was his favourite as it involved strategically grappling with the opponent and hitting the target and dodging the opponent with one's strength and skill. The match was won or lost only on the basis of these skills. Fortune does not play an important role in the game; on the contrary, immediate application of skills and running, efforts, swiftness, mental alertness play a deciding role in the game. Like a soldier in a war, in his school days, Bipin had occasion to participate in football competitions and he exhibited all these traits in the game.

Bipin had never aimed to be a footballer; he wanted to become an Army officer. Immediately after passing Class XII, Bipin had to clear the difficult exam of NDA (National Defence Academy). As such, the competitive examinations restricted his love for football. After passing Class XII in flying colours, he cleared both the medical and NDA examinations as per expectations, but as destined, be preferred his family tradition over the medical profession.

2nd Lieutenant with 'Sword of Honour'

Firm Determination—Resolute Decision

Bipin Rawat passed intermediate from Saint Edwards School in 1972-73. Later, though not only in his work field, but in the field of education, he achieved new heights and achievements, but he never forgot his school. In fact, he was deeply associated with Saint Edwards School. After taking over as COAS also, he visited the school as a guest. The COAS had intimate discussions with the students of the school, during which he advised them to make Army as their career. He told them that he had not chosen the military as a career due to family pressure, but this uniform had always been inviting him. There were other avenues for a profession or job, but he chose only what he loved. Joining the Army was his spontaneous decision and selection. Once, while addressing the youth, Bipin Rawat advised them to develop the ability to take right decisions and consider sticking to their right decisions as the most important discipline of life. "Take well-considered decision, implement it and support it honestly.

Firmly implement it and only then you would achieve success." After addressing the students, he signed the Visitor's Book, as per the tradition of the school, and wrote a message in the Visitor's Book. With his message, the Visitor's Book today is a pride possession for the college.

He used to narrate an incident about determination and firm decision, which was related to his entry into NDA. To cut the story short, "It was an interview to an important entrance test. Future of the career rested on that interview. I entered the room where the officer asked me some general questions and about my hobbies. I told him, that I loved trekking very much. Next question was fired, 'If you are going on a trek for four to five days in hills and jungle, then what is the one thing you would like to carry with you?' I thought for a few seconds and replied, 'I would keep a match-box with me.' Then, I was asked, 'Why that only?' I gave arguments in favour of my decision and said that the primitive man used to live in hills and jungles and fire was essential for him. 'With fire, I would be able to finish a number of important tasks, ranging from my own safety to sustenance.' In addition to this, I explained many values and uses of matches. The officers suggested certain other things, explained their usefulness in hills and jungles and also suggested other options and tried to pressurise me into changing my views, but I stuck to my decision. I didn't know that my decision was right or wrong, but probably the officers appreciated my resolute view and answer and I was selected to NDA."

Medal for Perseverance

After completing school education, Bipin Rawat proceeded to join the National Defence Academy, Khadakwasla. Located near Pune, the NDA is the first and only tri-Services academy in the world. This is the Defence Services Training Institute, where cadets of Army, Navy and Air Force undergo training jointly before being referred to the concerned Service academy for pre-commission training. Bipin Rawat started military education and training here itself. Then he went on to join the Indian Military Academy in order to enter the Indian Armed Forces. Spread over 1,400 acres, the IMA, the oldest military academy in the country, is located at Dehradun.

Second Lieutenant Bipin Rawat at IMA, with his maternal grandfather Thakur Kishan Singh and father Lt Gen Lakshman Singh

Apart from training the future military warriors in sports, adventure activities, physical training, exercises, weapons training and leadership development activities, the IMA, established in 1932, also conducts character-building activities. When passing through various courses, a cadet completes the training, he is given permanent commission as Lieutenant in the Army. After intermediate and passing the entrance exam of NDA, Bipin Rawat came to INA. This was all like a secondary education and he had still to go for higher education. The studious Bipin Rawat knew and believed that a capable officer should not only possess brilliant academic and educational qualifications, but he must also have higher degrees in military training. So far as his education and training at IMA were concerned, his performance was par excellence. He was honoured with the 'Sword of Honour'. During his tenure at NDA, Bipin Rawat was found to be lagging behind in the physical test, but with his courage and determination, he refused to give up and with his efforts and perseverance, he bagged the Gold Medal at the Indian Military Academy.

Training in Military Operations in America

After passing out of IMA, Rawat decided to join a course at United States Army Command and General Staff College at Fort Leavenworth in the USA. Established in 1881 by Wlliam Tekumseh Sheremon at Fort Leavenworth in Kansas, this staff college educates and trains international military officers. It conducts a ten months' graduate course, which covers leadership philosophy, military history, military strategic planning and directions for decision-making processes. Skill development and personality development of commanders and efficient and capable officers are the main subjects of the course. It imparts higher education about operational needs of the Army and art and science of using weapons. It has four schools and one of which provides specialised training in command and thus he did the 'higher command course' from this school. After learning various traits of military operations from the United States Army Command and General Staff College, Bipin Rawat returned home.

Rawat was also a graduate from Defence Services Staff College (DSSC), Wellington, one of the oldest military institutes. It was established as an Army Staff College at Deolali, near Nashik in 1905. It was shifted to Quetta, which is now in Pakistan, in 1907, but this happened before Independence. After partition of India and Pakistan in 1947, it returned to India as Army Staff College, at Wellington in Nilgiri district of Tamil Nadu. Wellington is a cantonment city of Conoor sub-division of Nilgiri district. Field Marshal Sam Manekshaw belonged to this place. Though Bipin Rawat had done academic graduation as B.Sc. and 'higher command course' from US Army Command and General Staff College, which was also a graduation course, but he decided to go in for graduation and post-graduation courses in military studies. In fact, DSSC is affiliated to Madras University, but it has also been recognised as a research centre since 1990. As such, Bipin Rawat, during his stay there, completed his MSc in 'Defence and Military Studies' and later took a diploma in management and computer studies alongwith MPhil degree. In 2011, he was awarded DPhil in military-media studies by Chaudhary Charan Singh University, Meerut. Besides, he participated in the higher command course at Mhow. Apart from his studious nature, he was a prolific writer also. In spite of his busy schedule, he penned a number of articles on national security and military leadership, which were published in various magazines and were highly appreciated by defence specialists. He was also a great orator. A number of his speeches and statements were widely talked of.

The Beginning of Military March

General Bipin Rawat was all of just 20 years, on 16 December, 1978, when he was commissioned in the 5th Battalion of Gorkha 11 Rifles as Second Lieutenant. After exactly two years, he got promoted to the post of Lieutenant on 16 December, 1980. When in 1984, he became Captain, he started getting recognition in his area. There must have been a number of marriage proposals, but Captain Rawat chose to marry Madhulika Rawat. Bipin Rawat and Madhulika, both belonged to different states. If we talk of prior to the creation of Uttarakhand, Bipin belonged to Uttar Pradesh, but it appears a little surprising that his wife had no connection with Uttarakhand. She was from Suhagpur in Shahdol district of Madhya Pradesh. She was the middle child of Mrigendra Singh, *ilakedar* of the area. Kunwar Mrigendra Singh was a descendant of the ruler of princely state of sub-division Suhagpur, of Shahdol district. He had been elected MLA from the Indian National Congress in 1967 and 1972. Suhagpur is a town in Hoshangabad district of Madhya Pradesh and a Nagar *panchayat*. Suhagpur is famous for its betel leaves, which are exported in large quantities to other countries. Madhulika was not born at her father's house in Suhagpur, but in Lucknow, at her maternal grandfather's house. Family environs of Madhulika were different from those of Bipin's.

Second Lieutenant General Bipin Rawat

The Marriage

Mrigendra Singh and Kunwar Mandhata Singh, ruler of Khairha Gadi state and his distant brother, had very cordial relations, so Mrigendra Singh asked him to look out for a suitable bridegroom for his daughter, Madhulika, who had passed out from Scindia Girls' School. Born at her maternal grandfather's house in 1969, Madhulika had passed intermediate from Gwalior's Scindia Girls' School and graduation in psychology from Delhi University. Then, Pratibha Singh, sister of Mandhata Singh was also married in the Banjara state of Uttarakhand and was living in Dehradun. She was related to Bipin Rawat through her in-laws. Pratibha Singh conveyed information about Bipin Rawat to the latter's brother. Bipin Rawat was a Captain in the Indian Army in those days. Thus Kunwar Mandhata Singh came to know about Bipin Rawat.

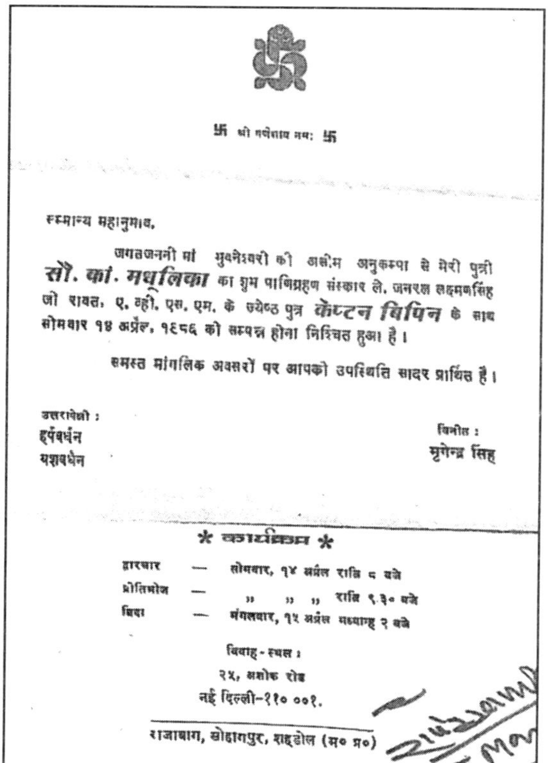

卐 श्री गणेशाय नमः 卐

सम्मान्य महानुभाव,

जगतजननी मां भुवनेश्वरी की असीम अनुकम्पा से मेरी पुत्री **सौ. कां. मधुलिका** का शुभ पाणिग्रहण संस्कार ले. जनरल लक्ष्मणसिंह जी रावत, ए. व्ही. एस. एम. के ज्येष्ठ पुत्र **कैप्टन बिपिन** के साथ सोमवार १४ अप्रैल, १९८६ को सम्पन्न होना निश्चित हुआ है।

समस्त मांगलिक अवसरों पर आपको उपस्थिति सादर प्रार्थित है।

उत्सुक :
हर्षवर्धन
यशवर्धन

विनीत :
मृगेन्द्र सिंह

* कार्यक्रम *

द्वारचार — सोमवार, १४ अप्रैल रात्रि ८ बजे
प्रीतिभोज — ,, ,, ,, रात्रि ९.३० बजे
विदा — मंगलवार, १५ अप्रैल मध्याह्न २ बजे

विवाह-स्थल :
२५, अशोक रोड
नई दिल्ली-११० ००१.

राजाबाग, सोहागपुर, शहडोल (म० प्र०)

Invitation card of Bipin-Madhulika's marriage

Bipin-Madhulika at the marriage ceremony

Yashwardhan Singh, brother of Madhulika Singh often tells that Bipin's father Lakshman Singh had himself, through a letter to Mrigendra Singh, proposed for the marriage of Madhulika with his son. The simplicity of Rawat family and behaviour of relatives had impressed all and they spontaneously liked Bipin Rawat. On the insistence of Kunwar Mandhata Singh and after Lakshman Singh's initiative in the form of a letter, the marriage proposal was finalised. There was a coincidence about their marriage, which is often talked about in the family as a 'pleasant coincidence'. The address of Madhulika's maternal grandfather in Lucknow was '25 Ashok Marg', whereas the house from where this marriage took place in Delhi was also '25 Ashok Road'.

Madhulika and Daughters

Daughters fondly remember their mother, Madhulika Rawat. For them, it is all unforgettable—how she brought them up, took their care and guided them at every step. All mothers must have been doing such things for their children, but for a mother, who was having bigger social responsibilities to cope with, whose husband also had almost been away from the family, must have been very difficult to provide such care to her daughters. Madhulika was very fond of social work. As she was living in a vast military society, for which her efforts may not have been sufficient, even then she undertook a number of social tasks. So far as her military society was concerned, the efforts she put in for the welfare of armymen, their wives, their children and dependants, were laudable and cannot be forgotten. She had been part of such efforts of social campaigns, which were started for the first time. During Bipin Rawat's tenure as COAS, Madhulika had been the chairperson of Army Wives' Welfare Association.

A non-profit organisation, the Army Wives' Welfare Association or AWWA was set up in 1966, with the objective of rehabilitation of war-widows and soldiers wounded in war. The Association also organises professional training for war-widows and empowers the beneficiaries. After the appointment of General Bipin Rawat as first CDS, Madhulika became chairperson of the Defence Wives' Welfare Association. This organisation has been engaged in laudable efforts for the welfare of husbands or wives of Army personnel and their children and other dependants. She launched a number of unique schemes for making wives of defence personnel economically independent and did excellent work in this direction. She was also associated with NGOs and welfare organisations, like '*Veer Naris*', which had been helping the widows, disabled children and cancer patients. After marriage, Madhulika spent many years away from husband, who had been posted to some of the most important difficult areas.

During this period, she took care of her two daughters—Kritika and Tarini. Later, the family accompanied Bipin Rawat to his place of posting.

Country First, then Family—Madhulika

"He was unaware that he was being promoted to COAS. When the phone started ringing, he realised something is brewing. Bipin never had time for us. During his posting to field areas, I had taken special care of my daughters. I lost many years in understanding Army life. I lived with my in-laws and children. When he became Army Commander, I accompanied him.

A divine couple

"After becoming COAS and later CDS, he used to leave his residence by 9.00 in the morning for his office in South Block and usually return to his family after 9.00 in the night. Saturdays and Sundays were not holidays for him. On these days, he used to meet various commands outside Delhi or officers and Jawans on the border. Normally, he did not always invite me to the normal programmes. My children always said, "We used to hanker for those movements when we all could spent sometime together with our children. He was too dedicated towards the country and Army. People used to praise his simplicity and connect with the children." In fact, he used to be very busy and could not spare time, but he had great affection for the children.

Bipin-Madhulika Rawat at the marriage ceremony

At the time of his elder daughter's marriage, he was Army Chief. I remember the simplicity with which he arranged the marriage ceremony in the Army House. All were witness to his simplicity. Younger daughter Tarini was practicing in a law firm. Tarini used to travel alone from Army House to Safdarjung by bus. Such small incidents indicate that Bipin never allowed his family to use his post or rank to influence others.

He never showed off. Reading and writing were his hobbies. He liked to travel within the country. When, during a foreign trip, people said how beautiful Switzerland is, he remarked, "These people have forgotten Kashmir." He loved his country very much.

After marriage, Bipin Rawat and Madhulika led their life together and in death also, they were together. Madhulika always complained that Bipin often did not take her along on his postings, but on the last journey, she was with him. From marriage to the last breath, like an ideal wife, Madhulika remained with General Bipin Rawat as his source of strength.

Tradition Broken

With the departure of Bipin Rawat, the tradition of sending a member of the family to Army has stopped as of now. Both daughters of Bipin Rawat and Madhulika Rawat, Kritika (1987) and Tarini (1993) chose their professions out of Army, according to their interests. Both of them had celebrity status due to their father General Bipin Rawat and mother Madhulika, but it may appear surprising that when needed, the media was unable to unearth significant information about them. Reason—both of them were usually very reserved. They never tried to take advantage of their father being the COAS or CDS. Like their father, they too never impressed others with their family background, fame, clout and capabilities. They never tried to take advantage of it and impress others with it; on the contrary, in deference to their dignity, both always behaved with simplicity and modesty. Apart from the family, some close relations and family friends, they were known only to the persons of their workplaces. In the world of today, where hunger for popularity and fame is forcing people to take to strange behaviour and performance, both these daughters of Bipin Rawat are far away from the most popular platform of social media. Elder daughter, Kritika is married and at present living in Mumbai, whereas younger, Tarini, is practicing as an advocate in Delhi. Both of them have been seldom seen publicly. People came to know about both of them when CDS Bipin Rawat and Madhulika Rawat died in a helicopter crash and their last rites were performed by both these daughters.

□

2
Battlefield
First General Directly Challenges China

During Bipin Rawat's tenure, India not only successfully displayed strong military deterrence against China, but forced China to submit and adopt a compromising attitude. Such a stance had never been witnessed prior to General Bipin Rawat.

Bipin Rawat's battalion was deployed on the front against the Chinese People's Liberation Army in 1986. He was the Company Commander when his battalion was deployed at the Line of Actual Control (LAC) on the border with China. During skirmishes in 1987, at Sumdorong Chu Valley, everyone witnessed the readiness of Bipin Rawat. But, after the 1962 war with China, this deadlock at the disputed McMahon Line was the first military confrontation and Rawat was directly handling the front. As a Major, he had commanded a company at Uri in Jammu & Kashmir. As a Colonel, he commanded his 5th Battalion of 11 Gorkha Rifles in Kibithu along the Line of Actual Control in the eastern sector. After General Manekshaw and General Dalbir Suhag, the third COAS from Gorkha Regiment Bipin Rawat had performed many valiant deeds during his tenure, but standoff with Chinese Army at Doklam was one of the most important events in his career. Such a strategic and diplomatic conduct with the Chinese had never been witnessed before.

Bipin Rawat taking salute as CDS

The Indian Army held ground when confronting the Chinese Army for 73 days. This incident and the strategy adopted by Bipin Rawat for this standoff had a number of strong diplomatic messages at international level. With this standoff, India ethically emerged victorious. This moral victory of India sent a message to India's other neighbours that India was not in favour of strengthening or maintaining military and economic relations with China at the cost of compromising its sovereignty and all must understand this stand of India. The message was clear particularly to India's neighbours, Sri Lanka and Bangladesh, who were facing a crisis due to economic agreements with China and it stressed on the need for them to reconsider their efforts to strengthen friendly relations with China and said that a strong and supportive friendly neighbour like India is always available for their help.

General Bipin Rawat had been the COAS for just six months. He was planning on essential changes in the Army, when once again China started behaving arrogantly on the north-eastern border of India. Indian Army got information about Chinese building a road in a village located on Doklam plateau, near the international border. Indian soldiers reached that village on Doklam on 16 June, 2017 and stopped the Chinese from building the road. They also confiscated Chinese bulldozers. China had been claiming to build the road in its own area, whereas India argued that the road construction work was being carried on in its friend Bhutan's area and it was strategically against India's interest. India strongly argued that it had the right to take action at that level under such circumstances. India was of the view that with such an activity, China was trying to alter the status quo situation of deployment of soldiers on India-China Actual Line of Control. India's viewpoint was quite clear that it would not allow China to construct the road. With this idea and strategy, India directly challenged China. This happened due to the boldness of General Bipin Rawat.

Taking charge as CDS, with the then COAS MM Narwane, Chief of Naval Staff Admiral Karamvir Singh and Chief of Air Staff Air Chief Marshal RKS Bhadoria

Diplomatic interventions led to the ending of China-India standoff on 28 August, 2017 which had started on 16 June, 2017. Both the countries agreed to withdraw their forces.

During this standoff, the Indian Army was fully prepared to take any action and on the international front, it presented itself as a strong, capable and professional Army in front of China's People's Liberation Army. Later, once again General Rawat had to face the Chinese challenge, when in May 2020, China tried to infiltrate in eastern Ladakh and both the countries had to face a bloody clash at Galwan. At that critical moment, General Bipin Rawat said in clear terms that after the incident at Galwan, the forces of both the countries had confronted each other a number of times. Both the countries do not want such close confrontations. If soldiers confront each other so often, chances of clashes would always be there. Our efforts should be to keep the soldiers apart from each other. It would be better if forces of both the countries were to revert to the situation prior to April 2020.

At some places in eastern Ladakh, the process of de-escalation or withdrawal has been slow. It is due to the permanent structures that China has constructed at the Line of Actual Control (LAC). Rawat's strategy was that under such circumstances, we too must not withdraw from these places. Under this strategy, we also constructed permanent structures in Ladakh. Both of us, China on other side and we on this side, have been firmly holding our grounds. Our forces would not withdraw from there. General Bipin Rawat had challenged that we are ready to reply to incidents like Galwan or any such misadventure and that China will receive a reply in the same language, if it tried to repeat such misplaced deeds like Galwan. Soldiers of both the countries were nearer to each other at Demchok in eastern area than in comparison to other places. When China continued with its arrogant behaviour, he started preparation for a possible war. It was dual responsibility—the first challenge was to keep the forces' morale high, while not creating any provocation for the other side. Then, in view of a possible war at the critical front in north-east, adequate deployment of forces was also necessary, so that India's preparation continued and internationally it would not be construed that India was creating war-like situation.

General Bipin Rawat had remarked that not Pakistan, but China was the foremost enemy of India. He truly believed that China is a bigger threat to us than Pakistan. In fact, Former Defence Minister George Fernandes too had expressed this opinion many years before. India's primary focus is on disengagement before de-escalation on the Line of Actual Control, as China is our number one enemy, not Pakistan. Rawat said that in time to come, India may have to face two enemies—China and China-supported Pakistan. He was of the opinion that China has been widely penetrating South Asia and the Indian Ocean to strengthen its claim to being an emerging world power. Chinese ingress into Myanmar and Bangladesh is against the Indian national interest as it amounts to an effort to surround India. The Chinese desire to become a world power poses a serious threat to political and military stability in South Asia.

CDS General Bipin Rawat had said that China was providing military aid to Pakistan to spread violence in PoK (Pakistan-occupied Kashmir). China's unhindered support to Pakistan is clearly an anti-India stance. Continuous investment in Myanmar is China's considered effort to weaken India's influence in Myanmar. This Chinese strategy is a great threat to the north-eastern states, which are an integral part of the country. After taking over as CDS, General Bipin Rawat had concluded that by 2030, China, India, Turkey and Indonesia would find a place in the top ten economies of the world. General Rawat's statement assured the common Indian that India was prepared to confront any situation with courage and capability.

Since the day General Bipin Rawat took over as CDS, he had been preparing all the three Indian Armed Forces, keeping in mind that India may have to face China and Pakistan on the battlefront simultaneously and then India should not be found lagging behind. He was assessing the requirements of the Indian Armed Forces in such an eventuality and with this in mind, he was making preparations. China and Pakistan had become aware of the aggressive strategy of General Rawat. Both the countries were terrified of the masterly military strategist, General Bipin Rawat, who was straightforward and used to challenge openly, as he had years of experience in counter-insurgency and high-altitude warfare and was an expert in the field.

Killing Terrorists in Their Den

Bipin Rawat was a synonym for fearlessness. He was a strong believer in finding solutions to problems through peace and negotiations, but for those who were adamant, he advocated the policy of entering their houses and killing them. This surgical strike was an example of this strategy.

Bipin Rawat amidst Jawans on the border

After the Pulwama attack, the world's attention was focussed on the deadlock between India and Pakistan. Then, the Indian Armed Forces, as a professional force, entered another country and struck at the terrorists. Earlier, on 4 June, 2015, Naga rebels killed 18 Indian Jawans of 6 Dogra

Regiment in an attack on Chandel in Manipur. Indian Army's rage flared up. When the Army launched a search operation, it was found that these rebels had crossed over to Myanmar to hide. Then, the Indian Army carried out counter-attacks across the border. Strict action was required against the rebel group to crush the rebels and raise the morale of the Army, while proving the might of the Army. After planning the operation, it was decided in a meeting with Rajnath Singh, Home Minister, Manohar Parrikar, the then Defence Minister, Ajit Doval, NSA, General Dalbir Singh Suhag, COAS and other officers on 4th June to give a crushing reply to the rebels. General Rawat was considered to be an expert in aggressive and foolproof strategy. 21 Para at Dimapur was under the control of 3rd Corps, which was now commanded by Bipin Rawat. As Chief of 3rd Corps of the Army, Lt Gen Rawat submitted a detailed plan of surgical strike against Naga rebels to Army Chief General Dalbir Singh Suhag within a few hours. It was a foolproof plan and success was guaranteed, as Bipin Rawat having rich experience of military operations for stopping the infiltration in north-east, had planned the surgical strike with detail and alertness.

The Myanmar Surgical Strike

The unit, responsible to carry out the strike, conducted a mock drill before the operation. Even mock camps were raised for the drill. The operation was rehearsed at mock camps. The Army had collected the input about camps of extremists' group, The National Socialist Council of Nagaland-Khaplang, at Ujia, near Ponue area of Myanmar. This place is close to the Manipur border. One terrorist camp had already been running in the border area in Myanmar territory. After the approval of Prime Minister Narendra Modi on 7 June, daredevil Jawans, divided into three groups and riding on a Dhruv helicopter, entered Myanmar territory on the night of 8-9 June and reached Nukluk through Chasad area of Ukhru. The operation started at 3.00 in the early morning. The camp was surrounded like the mock camp had been surrounded during the drill. After surrounding the camp, Jawans attacked the terrorists. Information about the progress of the operation was being continuously relayed to the Control Room in Delhi. Jawans chased out the terrorists from Ponue to Nukluk. In the meantime, information about fleeing of SS Khaplang, Chief of the National Socialist Council of Nagaland-Khaplang (NSCN) faction was received. However, with rocket launchers, the Army razed the camps of the terrorists. Within six days of the attack, the Myanmar base of NSCN was raided. It took the operation unit eight hours from leaving India and returning after completing the action, but the main action took just 40 minutes. The terrorist camp inside Myanmar territory was razed in just a single strike. International military community was surprised at the feat of carrying out the successful surgical strike and returning to their base.

General Bipin Rawat meeting the Jawans

Rawat—Master of Instant and Foolproof Planning

The 'Myanmar operation' was quite a different operation. The strategy of this operation was planned by Bipin Rawat within a few hours. Though planned in a short period, this was a solid plan which ensured its success. It was executed by

21 Para, part of the III Corps, which was under the strategist of this operation. Commandos for this operation had set forth in the uniform of Army's 12 Bihar Regiment, so that nobody could guess that they were not on a special operation, but were moving for routine operation. The strategy of Myanmar surgical strike of taking the enemy by surprise with a sudden attack proved highly successful. The unit, consisting of 70 Indian commandos from Manipur, entered Myanmar and crept up to the enemy's camp and attacked the Naga rebels, not allowing them any chance to escape. No Indian soldier was killed or wounded, whereas 38 Naga rebels were killed and seven wounded. Dozens of rebel bases were knocked down.

General Bipin Rawat with Ajit Doval, National Security Advisor

It was an important operation carried out by entering a foreign country under the command of Bipin Rawat. It sent a stern message to India's enemies. It was an open declaration of Indian Army's offensive defence strategy. Indian Army had made it clear that Indian forces, when required, would cross the Indian border and leave no stone unturned to destroy the enemy. Thereafter, a new slogan came into circulation, *'नया भारत है, घर में घुसकर मारेगा।'* (It is a new India which would kill by entering your house).

How Kaladan Project was Secured

Under Bipin Rawat, the armies of India and Myanmar carried out an important military operation on the Indo-Myanmar border for a fortnight and thwarted the rebels' planned attack on a mega structural project of India in the north-east. In fact, the Arakan Army was planning an attack on the Kaladan project, which is a transit project and would connect Kolkata's Haldia port to Sitwe port of Myanmar. On completion of this project, Mizoram would get connected to Myanmar. The importance of the project can be realised by the fact that it would reduce the distance between Myanmar and Mizoram by 1,000 kms. Moreover, travel time between both the places would also be reduced by at least four days. After getting inputs about a threat to the Kaladan project, the Army planned to attack the base of the rebels in Myanmar, south of Mizoram. In co-operation with the Myanmarese Army, the Indian Army launched an operation.

After taking over as COAS, General Bipin Rawat seen in the South Block courtyard

In the first phase of the operation, new rebel camps raised in border areas adjacent to Mizoram were destroyed and in the next phase, the camp of Naga group NSCN-Khaplng was targeted. The Indian Army also attacked the Arakan Army of Myanmar, which had been receiving support from Kachin Independence Army (KIA), which had imparted training to more than 3,000 combatants. This group is active in the Kachin province of Myanmar and which is adjacent to Chinese border where China is training them. These 3,000 ultras were trying to set up their base in Lawangtala district of Mizoram. The Army had launched the operation to chase away these rebels from this area. Now this area is under the control of the Myanmarese Army. A special force of the Army, Assam Rifles and other infantry units were involved in this operation.

Advice against China's Shrewdness

Speaking at the webinar on 'Opportunities and Challenges in North-Eastern India' organised by the *Indian Military Review*, General Rawat had said that after a military coup in Myanmar, international sanctions have been imposed against it. Amidst these international sanctions, China has strengthened its efforts to make inroads in Myanmar with a view to accelerate the pace of implementation of its project, 'Belt and Road Initiative'. China would be strictly watching India from Myanmar. As India's north-east area is connected with the rest of the country through the narrow and vulnerable Siliguri corridor of 'Chicken Neck', this area has 'extreme geo-strategic importance' and which China has been eyeing covertly. Under such circumstances, internal security and its challenges have 'serious international dimensions'. Keeping security challenges in sight, it would be important to make the Central and State Security Forces more alert and vigilant and strengthen it through regional and international diplomatic strategic support. During Bipin Rawat's tenure, 'continuous anti-terrorist operations' in the north-eastern region and destruction of 'safe havens' for extremist organisations in neighbouring countries like Bangladesh, Bhutan and Myanmar have led to a considerable decline in violence. Presence of Rohingya refugees is also another 'emerging area of concern' for this region. General Rawat said that these refugees could be used by radical Islamic groups for spreading unrest and weakening peace and security. Apart from China, the border situation in the north-east can lead to another security concern due to rebel activities, infiltration and drug trafficking.

At present, we need to consolidate and strengthen these positive activities with peace talks. 'Return to normalcy' in Myanmar would be beneficial to India, particularly to the region, due to 'our historical and cultural relations' with the country. Bipin Rawat's vision regarding safety-security concerns of north-east and the successful military actions he took in the north-east are praiseworthy and memorable.

General Bipin Rawat at Air Force Day parade

General Teaching Lesson to Pakistan

General Rawat was a General with a new vision. He played an important role in making the Indian Army more aggressive. During his career, ranging four decades, the aggressive stance Rawat gave to the Indian Army was unprecedented. The Army intruded from PoK to Myanmar and killed the enemies. He told me in an interview that the war of new age is not fought only in the field and as such, the Indian Armed Forces will have to be more proficient strategically. Alongwith traditional war, he had a vision for the Army to be proficient in psychological, cyber and legal warfare.

Surgical Strike in Balakot

Pakistan-trained terrorists attacked the Indian Army camp at Uri in Jammu & Kashmir, near the LoC on 18 September, 2016. The sleeping Jawans were targeted in this terror strike, in which 17 of them lost their lives. It was the biggest terror attack on Indian Army in two decades. In another terror attack at Pulwama in Jammu & Kashmir, more than 40 Jawans were martyred. The Indian Army carried out a counter attack after the terror strike on Army camp at Uri and CRPF camp in Pulwama.

General Bipin Rawat with Prime Minister Narendra Modi

The surgical strike after Uri terror attack in 2017, in which the Army entered the Pak-occupied Kashmir and attacked the launching pads of terrorists, was primarily planned by Rawat. During his tenure as COAS in 2018, General Bipin Rawat had said, "India needs to launch one more surgical strike." General Bipin Rawat was COAS, when in retaliatory action, the Indian Army entered PoK on the midnight of 28-29 September, 2019 and targeted a terrorist training camp of Jaish-e-Mohammed at Balakot, in an aerial attack through a surgical strike. The Indian Army announced on 29 September, 2019 about it entering PoK and attacking the terror launching pads and damaging terrorists' camps. After the surgical strike, in a talk with the media, Bipin Rawat called this strike as a message to Pakistan and said, "We want to tell that more such operations could follow."

In the surgical strikes on the terror camps in Pakistan-occupied Kashmir, the Army killed many terrorists. This strike established India as a country capable of taking a big and decisive action against terrorists in the world. The blueprint for this strike was chalked out by General Rawat, who was Lt Gen at that time. Charting a successful strategy of entering two different countries—Myanmar and Pakistan (PoK), General Rawat proved his unique vision on the battlefront. When he said, "India is prepared to fight on two-and-a-half fronts," he made it clear that India had started working on a different kind of warfare. He meant that India had to remain prepared for maintaining internal security in addition to the two fronts with China and Pakistan. The Army has also adopted such a strict stance against terrorism in Jammu & Kashmir. The Army has been winning the hearts of Kashmiris; on the other hand, terrorists are being dealt with mercilessly. Bipin Rawat had said that when we talk of Jammu & Kashmir, we include PoK and Gilgit also. Without naming Pakistan, General had stated that because of illegal occupation by our neighbour, the PoK is a land of illegal occupation. He also said the the region being illegally occupied by Pakistan is not under the control of Pakistan but is being administered by the terrorists. PoK is a country, which is being controlled by the terrorists. Pakistan would also continue its proxy war in Jammu & Kashmir. Not only this, Pakistan would also create problems in other parts of the country, towards which it is striving.

CDS General Bipin Rawat had also said that if Pakistan wants peace, then the ceasefire would have to be maintained for a long time as it would be in the interest of both the countries. The CDS said that there had been a number of ceasefire violations during the last few years, in which not only small arms, but high-calibre weapons were used. These ceasefire violations have caused considerable damage to the defensive structure of the Pakistani Army. Its soldiers have been killed or wounded in large numbers. On a number of occasions, in a clear message to Pakistan, CDS Bipin Rawat had said that countries sponsoring terrorism must be blacklisted by FATF (Financial Action Task Force), global money laundering and terror financing watchdog, and isolated diplomatically. He said that boys and girls of 10-12 years of age are being radicalised, which is a matter of greater concern.

With the then Defence Minister, Nirmala Sitaraman

After the occupation of Afghanistan by Taliban, Bipin Rawat had said that India had anticipated the rule of Taliban in Afghanistan and for that, India was ready with a plan. He said that India was prepared for any situation in Afghanistan. If the situation there had any impact on India, Indian Army was prepared to face it. It would be dealt with the way terrorism is treated. The pace of events in Afghanistan was definitely surprising, because India had anticipated that it would take two months' time for occupation of Afghanistan by Taliban. But, all this happened unexpectedly fast.

'Operation All Out'

General Rawat had a vast experience of high-altitude battlefields and managing anti-terror operations. The most important responsibility for him was to bring the situation in Kashmir under control. Under such circumstances, the decision to roll out 'Operation All Out' was taken. General Rawat was behind this operation. He considered instilling fear in the minds of the terrorist cadre necessary to defeat terrorism. He said that if anybody took to the gun, the Army would reply in that language only. This operation continued till 2019 and the security forces succeeded in breaking the back of the Kashmir module of Lashkar-e-Taiba and Jaish-e-Mohammed to a great extent.

Talking to the media

'Operation All Out' was launched after the death of eight pilgrims and injury to 18 during the Amarnath *yatra*. For the 'Operation All Out', which was started in 2017 to deal with the terrorists in Jammu & Kashmir, a joint team was constituted, which consisted of CRPF, J&K Police, BSF and Intelligence Bureau along with the Indian Army. A message was sent that security would be provided to persons giving information about terrorists and taking action against terrorists. 'Operation All Out' targeted terror outfits, like Lashkar-e-Taiba, Jaish-e-Mohammed, Hizbul Mujahideen and Al-Badr.

During his tenure, General Rawat toured Jammu & Kashmir extensively. He visited forward military posts to strengthen the morale of the Jawans. He once warned the terrorists entering from Pakistan that they would cross the border on two legs and return on four shoulders. "They would come and we would be dispatching them under the ground." General Rawat's strong message was a green signal for the Army. The impact of continuous action against infiltration by terrorists and cross-border firing was being clearly seen in those days. General Rawat had said with reference to the locals that they would 'lynch terrorists'. This was a positive sign. Regarding human rights, he had said, "How can killing of a terrorist be violation of human rights? If any terrorist is operating in your area, why would you not kill him?" CDS was of the opinion, "You will have to create fear among terrorists that before you kill us, we'll kill you."

After repealing of Article 370, through his intelligence he kept the situation in Kashmir under his control. He maintained normalcy in Kashmir with heavy deployment of Army. During this period, he kept the situation in full control by overseeing deployment of Jawans at LoC and in the plains through coordination.

□

3

Work-Field

General for Major Transformation

CDS Bipin Rawat was proficiently practical and firm on principles. He was quite tactful and social also. He achieved remarkable success in his operational area due to a harmonious mix of these traits.

I met General Bipin Rawat in 2009 for the first time. In those days, I was with 'Sahara Samay TV Channel'. Being given the defence beat, I was a regular visitor to South Block. I was in Army Headquarters, South Block on that day when I met Col Ajay Kothiyal, Commanding Officer of Garhwal Regiment. He was slated to proceed on the Satopant mountaineering expedition. While walking in the South Block corridor, he introduced me to Bipin Rawat, who had been recently promoted to Major General. It was a brief meeting of about two to four minutes. When we were coming out of South Block after meeting him, Col Ajay Kothial told me, "Manjeet, Major General Bipin Rawat is a thorough professional and a righteous officer. He is likely to become Army Chief one day." His prophecy came true in the year 2016, when the government handed over to him the post of Army Chief, superseding two Lieutenant Generals.

With General Dalbir, after taking over as Army Chief

After the Meeting

After that brief meeting in 2009 and talks with Col Ajay Kothial, there was inadvertently an imprint of General Rawat in my mind and during my tenure in Delhi, I continuously followed his work and his postings. With his becoming Major General and then Lt General and then appointment as Corps Commander in north-east, when he became the Army Commander of Southern Command and was posted at Pune, I contacted him for a programme being organised in Delhi. It was a community programme of people from Uttarakhand. Since he belonged to Uttarakhand, I invited him for this special programme, but unfortunately he could not attend it. While returning after Delhi Commanders' Conference, he himself called me and regretfully informed me that due to an appointment with Army Chief, General Dalbir Suhag, he would not be able to attend the programme, but we would soon meet. His absence at the programme was a disappointment, but his assurance of meeting soon proved a boon as it led to a chain of meetings which continued till his demise. After a few meetings as a journalist, with his sociable and courteous behaviour, such meetings led to family relations between us. My earlier meetings resulted in family relations with him by the time he was appointed Vice Chief. He always visited us, whenever I invited him to any personal or social function. My daughter Sara's birthday celebration was the first family programme in which he participated, alongwith his wife Madhulika Rawat. General Rawat was bestowed with the quality of adjusting himself according to the atmosphere. I remember seeing him become a child with the children at the birthday party of my daughter. He was old with elders and child with children. Such was General Bipin Rawat bestowed with an unparalleled quality of winning hearts.

Author Manjeet Negi with General Bipin Rawat

I remember when I heard the news of his becoming Army Chief, I was at the temple of Pitambara Mai in Datia and I took *prasad* for him. When I telecast this news around 9.00 at night, a number of people rang me up. Next morning, after reaching Delhi, I headed for the residence of General Rawat, but he was not at home. I gave the *prasad* to his wife Madhulika and told her about my visit to the Pitambara Mai temple and bringing this *prasad*. Subsequently I took the first interview of his wife on her husband becoming the Army Chief. This was the first interview of Madhulika to the media. At least she was talking on TV for the first time. During the interview, she shared certain family and household matters. She explained how she played her role in the life of Bipin Rawat, how she carried out all her duties, like taking care of father-in-law and mother-in-law and children, bringing up both the daughters and providing a conducive atmosphere to enable her husband to reach new heights in his career. Emboldened by her inspiring efforts, he was continuously touring the border areas in difficult times too.

Rawat in a New Avatar

I noted a great change in General Bipin Rawat's modus operandi after becoming Army Chief. Earlier he was a placid person and was not much communicative to the media, but after becoming the Army Chief, a new *avatar* of General Rawat emerged. He used to talk to the media with confidence about matters related to the country and the Army. I almost had talks with him daily. After taking over as COAS, he dedicated his whole life to the Army and the country. He used to work on Saturdays and Sundays; also on official holidays of the government. He told me that he would try to visit the border or to a place or military base, where he could meet more and more Jawans and military officers. For this, he often used to travel by plane or helicopter to such places, instead of spending holidays for relaxing or attending some family programmes. During these regular meetings, he used to present his arguments regarding the changes he was seeking in the Army and used to get feedback from them. During his tenure as Army Chief and when he became CDS, I had interviewed him a number of times for the TV channel 'Aaj Tak'. As the Army Chief, he planned a number of important operations. Under 'Operation All Out', terrorists in Jammu & Kashmir were dealt with firmly. Not only hundreds of terrorists were killed, but a campaign to bring them to mainstream was also planned. He warned the infiltrating terrorists that if they entered Kashmir by crossing the border with weapons, they were destined to dig their own graves. Although he had been criticised for some of his statements and actions, he never backtracked from his statements. He did and said only what he believed in with his mind and heart.

Preparing for a flight on LCA 'Tejas'

I had always noticed that doors of his house, Army House, were always open to any person, journalist or leader from Jammu & Kashmir. Similarly, he never hesitated in meeting any person or politician coming from any part of the country. He used to talk openly on all matters and he would leave an indelible print of a leader, away from the Army, on the people he met. Whenever I visited his residence, which was usually on Saturdays or Sundays, I noticed that he would meet and share his views with people, whether they were politicians or social workers or experts in some field, provided he was at home and not in a hurry to participate in an Army programme or meeting

Jawans and the officers or to an event of his liking. He always tried to learn newer things, ranging from agriculture to science and techonology or defence field. He always laid emphasis on familiarising himself with new technologies during his visits to Defence Expo, Air Show or any defence exhibition.

Criticising DRDO

When Prime Minister Narendra Modi launched the campaign 'Make in India', General Rawat was the pioneer in advocating it. He made every possible effort to provide opportunities in the defence sector to Indian companies on indigenous techniques. He criticised DRDO on this matter on various occasions. He was of the view that DRDO must concentrate on construction of large military equipments, like missiles and naval ships, machines, weapons and avoid manufacturing of small arms, bullet-proof jackets and all other general parts for Indian companies. And he used to put his views about this firmly in meetings and outside meetings. He used to meet indigenous companies in different parts of the country and seek their feedback. After becoming Chief of Defence Staff, he wanted to continue vigorously with his plan of establishing a theatre command among the three Services and their integration. He wanted to implement this plan within a definite time-limit. He was holding discussions regarding this with the three Services and in the initial stages, he had to face disagreement between Army and Air Force over this matter. Though he could not fulfil his last and most important defence ambition, he drew near to fulfilling his ambitious plans, whether they related to 'theatre command and integration' or 'indegenous' or 'Make in India' in the defence services.

Visionary of 'Make in India' in Defence Services

Bipin Rawat visualised coordination and co-operation among all the organs of military and their becoming self-dependent. He put in his best efforts to persuade all the three forces to adopt 'Make in India' and use 'Make in India' equipment as soon as possible.

CDS Bipin Rawat was not only a great warrior and war-winner, he was also a winner of hearts. Those who had worked with him or officers who had come into his contact during his tenure were highly appreciative of his efficiency, but they also could never forget to mention his humane and sociable behaviour. Not only I, but even Rear Admiral Om Prakash Singh Rana (retired), decorated with AVSM, VSM, was highly impressed by him within a few meetings. The first meeting between Rear Admiral Rana with Bipin Rawat took place when General Bipin Rawat was appointed COAS. At that time, Rear Admiral Rana was Director General, Naval Armament Inspector at the naval headquarters. Bipin Rawat's father General Lakshman Singh Rawat and father-in-law of Rear Admiral Rana, Commandant Rajendra Singh Negi (village Sula, Patti Aswalashu) were educated together at Jahrikhal. As such, he had some information about General Rawat's family and background, but after some meetings in Delhi and talking with each other, he was deeply impressed with Bipin Rawat's excellent personality and ideology. He says, "He was a genius person, valiant soldier, educationist, an able professional military leader, a person with deep thinking and endowed with remarkable vision. Rawat was not only a true patriot, but a nationalist and a strong advocate of self-dependent India." Military service at home and abroad, selection for outstanding courses in service career and national and international medals and honours are ample proofs of his being virtuous, able and great character. He had also been decorated with medals like Param Vishisht Seva Medal, Ati Vishisht Seva Medal, Padma Vibhushan, Uttam Yudh Seva Medal, Operation Parakram Medal and Videsh Seva Medal. For his distinct service to the nation, US Army Command and General Staff College included him in the 'International Hall of Fame', which is a great honour for the country and the Army.

With the then Naval Chief Admiral Karamvir Singh, Army Chief General MM Narvane and Air Force Chief Air Chief Marshal RKS Bhadoria

During my many meetings with him, I realised that his perspective about national strategic security was crystal clear. As such, he stressed upon making and following policies against anti-India countries with the co-operation of the present government and political leadership and, before adopting such policies, to consider about the possibilities of fighting war in two geographical regions simultaneously and to devise plans to counter such a situation. It was General Rawat who presented the outline of policies regarding jointness of forces and organised them in five independent theatre commands, playing an important role in finalising their short-term and far-reaching programmes and preparing guidelines for their implementation.

Guided Army on Self-dependence

General Rawat particularly stressed upon the security aspect as progress in this direction had always been fluctuating. If we consider the defence production in the country, we would find that during the 19th century, the British founded ordnance factories at Nilgiri, Jabalpore and Calcutta with the aim of assuring a regular supply of weapons to forces in the Pacific Ocean and Southeast Asia against their enemies. After Independence, the production of these factories went down as the government of the time believed in better political, social and trustworthy relations with the neighbouring countries. Possibly, national security lost its importance due to the order of precedence in this attempt and process. But Chinese aggression in 1962, the Cold War and the US supply of arms and ammunition to Pakistan led to concern for our national security. India signed a strategic agreement with the then Soviet Union, under which Soviet Union supplied arms and armaments in large numbers. With these weapons, we were able to modernise our Armed Forces to a great extent. The modernisation of forces led to strengthening the military capabilities beyond expectation. Later, the country started production of defence equipment.

Importance of self-dependence in defence production need not be underlined. It has become much too important and we are also aware of this fact, yet why we failed to make the required progress in this field? May be this could be due to insufficient research and defence material, lack of basic infrastructure for production of arms and armaments and other priorities of the government. In due course, there would be expansion of ordnance factories, public sector enterprises, technical and educational institutions, DRDO, etc. and indigenisation of defence materials too was in progress, yet we were forced to import large quantities of most of the defence materials. Developing this field with the help of world-class educational and technical educational institutes, laboratories with deep research facilities, ordnance factories, public sector enterprises, large private companies and thousands of micro, small and medium enterprises in the country and related government plans are positive policies. All these jointly establish India as a hub of modern research and production as they create a proper eco-system for indegenisation. These governmental efforts have started showing results.

With Defence Minister Rajnath Singh

The country has made considerable progress in the field of indegenisation. It includes naval ships, traditional and atomic submarines, '*Arjun*' tanks, light combat aircraft, hi-tech and advanced light helicopter, '*Varunastra*' torpedo, mines, explosives, guns, various weapons, rocket launchers, Agni, Prithvi, B-5, K-4 and air-to-air, air-to-surface, surface-to-air missiles. Anti-tank '*Nag*' missile, cruise missile 'Brahmos', 'Kavach' anti-missile system, sonar, radar, combat management system with communication network, electronic warfare, heavy engineering, etc are also made in India. Besides, a number of state-of-the-art ordnance systems are being developed in India and this journey of indigenisation is continuing. If we take a look at the modern perspective of self-dependence in security, we find an effective roadmap.

Bipin Rawat must be remembered for his initiative in the direction of joint defence research by Indian and foreign companies under strategic partnership and production of defence equipment under 'Make in India' or devising successful defence purchase and production policies or converting ordnance factories into seven public sector units with the aim of strengthening their capacity. Besides, Bipin Rawat also contributed to imposing government restrictions over the import of 'military sub-systems' and the development of space-based sensors, drone, directed energy and electromagnetic weapons, artificial intelligence, Internet of Things, cyber security, nanotechnology, etc. Even his contribution towards latest applications in security communication-based space technology, networking, intelligence, remote sensing, anti-ballistic missile defence, global positioning and navigation is also memorable.

Addressing Jawans on the front

Wednesday, the 8 December, 2021—a sad day in the history of Indian Army. CDS Bipin Rawat and his wife Madhulika Rawat were travelling to Defence Services Staff College in Wellington from Sulur Airbase by IAF helicopter MI-17V5. The helicopter crashed in Coonoor hills of Nilgiri district. All persons aboard the helicopter, except Group Captain Varun Singh, were killed. The seriously injured Group Captain later succumbed to his injuries after a few days of struggle. In this tragic incident, the country lost its first Chief of Defence Staff, the topmost post in the Indian Armed Forces.

Architect of Military Modernisation

Apart from liberating the Indian Army from the customs followed by the British Army, this Army Chief had been the pioneer in positive changes and technological revolutions in the Army. Bipin Rawat concentrated on preparing the military for fighting future wars. Indigenisation, modernisation, theatre command were parts of this strategy.

General Rawat told me about a meeting with the Prime Minister during which the latter's words led him to contemplate deeply. He had said, "General Rawat, we are prepared to make all efforts to modernise the military, but I fail to understand, why there is an exemption given on liquor of foreign companies? Why should the country's taxpayer's money be used for purchasing foreign liquor? Why should we allow the foreign liquor companies to earn huge profits?" General Rawat told me, "Prime Minister's concern had a deep impact on my mind. When I returned to my office, I issued an order giving strict instructions for ban on foreign liquor. I knew that this decision of mine would not be acceptable to many, who would criticise me. My decision was opposed fiercely in all the three forces. Most of them were not aware that I had implemented this decision first on myself and I removed all liquor of foreign brand from my house."

As a writer and journalist, I noticed on many occasions that thereafter, General Rawat never himself used foreign liquor, nor allowed it to be used in military canteens and messes.

Similarly, General Rawat restricted the use of luxury cars in the Armed Forces as military canteens allowed huge concessions on costly Indian and foreign cars. When the concession was stopped, this decision of his too was subjected to massive opposition. General Rawat took all these hard decisions with a view to inculcate ethics in the forces and soldiers and to establish higher standards for indigenisation. The most important thing was that he implemented these decisions first on himself. Under these decisions, General Rawat also banned stay of military officers in expensive hotels. He felt that staying in luxury hotels is expression of unnecessary elitist tendency and extravagance. He said that except for unavoidable and urgent reasons or work, military officers should stay in messes in order to save the exchequer revenue and lead to better coordination and connect of officers with their subordinates.

Making Military more Lethal

General Bipin Rawat submitted to the government a plan for large-scale reorganisation of the military at a time when most of the budget allocation was limited to payment of salaries. It was a revolutionary idea of minimising the size of the military and turn it into a more smart and lethal force. It was visualised that though it would be reduced in size, but it would be a more active, swift and effective force. Under this proposal, the number of officers and ORs was to be reduced by 50,000 in the first phase. General Rawat had suggested integrating Military Secretariat and Directorate of Perspective Plan into one unit. To start with, the Directorate General of Rashtriya Rifles was to be transferred to Jammu & Kashmir, Directorate of Military Training to Military Training Command to Shimla and integrating Information System and Information Technology Directorates.

He also suggested abolition of the Brigadier post in the Army. General Rawat believed that with the reorganisation of the Army, at least 300 high-ranking military officers from Delhi could be rendered surplus. In the first phase of reorganisation, reduction of 50,000 officers and Jawans could easily be effected in the almost 13-lakh strong Army. In the next phases, this reduction could reach around one-and-a-half lakh. Undoubtedly, in this new age, all things have become more effective and capable in smaller sizes and technologically-improved versions. It would be more feasible to integrate different departments with similar mandate into a combined department, which would not only be convenient for sharing resources, equipment and command and control, but the integrated efforts would lead to better and quick results. Such a vision was possible by a visionary like General Rawat.

Revolutionary Idea of Direct Recruitment of JCOs

General Rawat had several plans about the future Indian Army. He submitted a proposal for direct recruitment of Junior Commissioned Officers (JCOs) to attract young officers in the Army. This would allow the Army to get young and middle-aged officers for campaigns against terrorism and other operations. He suggested to the Adjutant General Branch about recruitment of those candidates as JCOs, who had failed to join as Army officers due to shortage by 5 marks. If the Army recruits a skilled IT engineer as JCO, then his or her services could be utilised for cyber operations and cyber warfare. They could be provided with a secured job at an initial monthly salary of Rs. 70,000.

With this revolutionary proposal of General Rawat, the possibilities for attracting more youth towards Army seemed practicable. In the Army, however, it takes almost 20 years for a Jawan to become a Junior Commssioned Officer. During a war or anti-terror operations, JCOs act as the link between the Jawans and officers. If this proposal gets accepted, then there would be considerable reduction in the period of becoming a JCO. In any difficult situation, they too could lead the operation if officers are not available to take the lead. If General Rawat's proposal is implemented, then directly recruited JCOs could become officers within a minimum span of time and even reach to the rank of Lieutenant Colonel.

Abolition of Customary Orderlies and Assistants

General Rawat had realised that almost 2,000 Jawans had been working as assistants in former officers' residences. On investigation, it was found that about 1,000 Jawans (equal to a battalion in the Army) were working as assistants in the residences of former Army officers at NOIDA, Gurgaon and Greater Noida—areas adjacent to Delhi. Jawans, in similar numbers, have also been deployed in the residences of former Army officers in other parts of the country. General Rawat considered this a misuse of Jawans trained for war. He announced the decision to abolish the custom of providing assistants to former Army officers. As expected, his decision was criticised and former Army officers were annoyed and felt uncomfortable.

At the front with Defence Minister

He recounts an incident. One evening, when he returned from office, wife of former Army Chief, General Sunderji, came to meet him with a complaint. She said that with the removal of assistants, the Army had created a great problem for former Army officers and this was completely a wrong decision. How would they live without assistants? These assistants were doing a lot of work in their residences; now, who would carry out these jobs? "I told her, an assistant would suffice for your household, who could cook your morning food and when required, he would drive your vehicle, as Armymen are experts in every field. Then General Sunderji's wife asked, 'If there are guests in the house, then who would cook food for them?' She also talked about a number of such trivial issues and asked me to reconsider my decision. She had come to my residence at about 8.30 in the evening and I had not even removed my uniform. I gave her all sorts of arguments about the benefits of reducing the number of assistants, feasibility and advantages to the Army and the country, but she continued to insist on rollback of the decision citing reasons like inconvenience, helplessness, etc.

Taking over as the first CDS of the country

"It was midnight and the discussion was continuing. I asked her to have food and then we would continue the

Bipin Rawat to look into the matter, he promptly replied that it was not possible as it would become a precedent and in future, there would be many such matters, wherein families of soldiers would demand a special plane. Thus, General Rawat, in a sense, over-ruled Defence Minister Rajnath Singh's decision.

Highest Priority to Indigenisation

For decades, there have been demands for some important changes in the Army to facilitate its further modernisation. It was a very complicated and hard task, which could only be undertaken by an energetic and dedicated person with innovative vision. When Bipin Rawat became Army Chief, he did not waste his time in big talk but proceeded to institute certain important changes that he had already been thinking and visualising in the Army. He wanted India to work towards 'Make in India' and stop import of weapons. General Rawat had been making continued efforts to adopt latest technologies for manufacturing improved and modern weapons for the Army. Under General Bipin Rawat as CDS, the 'strategic partnership model' was applied for upgrading weapons for the Army. Under this model, the government permitted private companies to jointly produce fighter jets, helicopters, submarines and tanks through collaboration with foreign weapon producers. Thus his push and ensuing contribution towards modernisation of defence manufacturing cannot be forgotten.

General Rawat always stressed upon a strong and domestic defence industrial base, as this was the only alternative for India. He sugessted initially that weapons with lesser technical specifications could be produced indeginously. "We must encourage 'Make in India' and build a strong foundation for our industry. If they deliver 70 per cent of General Staff Qualitative Requirements (GSQR), then they should be provided with an opportunity. It means that in the initial stage, if they are a little inferior in quality, we must accept it as, with experience and

With young women officers of the Air Force

General Rawat took strict action against two Major Generals posted in Lucknow; he also resolved the dispute between two Lt Generals, also in Lucknow. An NCC cadet had complained against Major General Dr Subhash Chandra, a former ADG, NCC in Gujarat, of posting obscene messages on mobile. When the Major General took charge of ADG of UP, NCC, a 'court of enquiry' was instituted against him. Meanwhile, he was attached to the Army Recruitment Headquarters. After declaring him guilty in the enquiry, Major General was dismissed from service.

General Rawat also ordered enquiry into the matter related to giving permission for the construction of a bungalow by a GoC. Even after retirement, a 'court of enquiry' and 'summary of evidence' by the Army was completed at Danapur, against this officer of the rank of Major General. A dispute between Lt Gen Alok Singh Kler, General Officer Commanding in Chief of South-Western Command and Lt Gen KK Repswal, Chief of Staff over authority had continued for seven months. General Bipin Rawat ordered an enquiry into the matter by the then Chief of Central Command in Lucknow, Lt Gen Iqroop Singh Ghuman. After the 'court of enquiry', the dispute was resolved.

Towards Military Theatre Commands

Although the constitution of a Unified Theatre Command for three forces could not be completed before his untimely death, the process for military unification had started under his leadership. India fought the Kargil war in 1999 with Pakistan after which, a number of committees had submitted their proposals for constitution of the Theatre Commands and the post of Chief of Defence Staff. After 20 years, on 15 August, 2019, announcing the creation of the post of Chief of Defence, Prime Minsiter Narendra Modi had said, "Coordination exists among the three forces and all of them are working for modernisation in their own way, but in view of the changing spheres and nature of wars and increasing role of technology, compartmentalised thinking for India would not be feasible. The country would have to surge forward with complete unified military power. And with this in mind, this post is being created."

General Bipin Rawat with Prime Minister Narendra Modi

General Bipin Rawat was appointed the first Chief of Defence (CDS) of the country on 31 December, 2019, to carry out the important task of reorganisation of the three Armed Forces. His most important mandate was to implement jointness and integration of the three Services. In addition to this, he was given the responsibility of reorganisation of the three Services and creation of 'Theatre Command' within three years. He was working on an important and ambitious 'Theatre Command Project', which was to play an important role in combating the danger lurking from Pakistan and China.

In fact, the 'Theatre Command' is useful during the war, when jointness and integration are established among the three Service Chiefs so that they can share their information, resources and strategies for confronting the future security challenges. Strategies chalked out with the help of the 'Theatre Command' facilitate successful and effective strike against the enemy. The resources and weapons of all the three forces can be utilised against different targets or jointly on a single target. Thus, it results in manifold increase in the capability of the forces.

At present, the forces have a strength of almost 15 lakhs and to organise and unify this strength, a 'Theatre Command' is required. With a single command, the expenses on modernisation of the forces would be minimised. Under such circumstances, only one force would not be benefitted by any modern technique, but all forces under the umbrella would stand to benefit by it. CDS General Bipin Rawat was working on four 'Theatre Commands' for which the target of constituting these commands by 2022 was decided.

Due to his sudden demise, he could not achieve his target, but he did create three big agencies for unification of the three forces. First was the Cyber Defence Agency, second was Defence Space Agency and third, Special Operation Division. In the near future, these could be converted into separate commands. Nine months after CDS General Rawat's death, a new CDS has been appointed. CDS Rawat was working at several levels, towards reforms of the military and which included the 'Theatre Command'. It is not going to be easy for our new CDS keeping in mind how much of work has to be done on these fronts.

Challenging Baton to New CDS

The government is very much interested in the 'Theatre Commands'. After CDS Rawat's sudden demise, the priority of the new CDS General Anil Chauhan is to expedite the process of achieving the creation of 'Theatre Commands'. His second priority would be to prepare the military for future wars and accordingly, there will be other areas which will require his attention, which will also include the procurement list of all the three divisions of the forces. Budget demands of each division of the military will have to be rationalised and start the common purchase at the earliest. The demand list of each division of the military believing in single-handed purchase will have to be pruned. I have written already how it is very expensive to purchase same defence equipment separately for each Armed Force! Fighting jointly under the common campaign plan in any future war would also have to be ensured. There appeared bitterness among the three forces during the tenure of General Rawat and which has to be removed and it would also to be ensured that the three divisions of the military do not thrust their wills on the headquarters. CDS Anil Chauhan is a man of few words but he is a very sharp and firm person. He will have to think in entirety with the point of view of all the three Services and out of his own uniform. He will also have to ensure the continuance of *Lakshman rekha* between the government and the highest military post.

Darling of the Jawans

General Rawat, who had been advising the Jawans on *naam* (honour), *namak* (loyalty), *nishan* (identity), *wafadari* (trust) and *izzat* (respect), motivated them with his own example and became a darling of the Jawans.

General Rawat was very popular among his former officers, the then juniors and even among the Jawans and there were several reasons for this popularity. When he took over as COAS, he phoned all retired Generals and wives of all deceased former

Receiving VSM from the-then
President of India, Ramnath Kovind

At the Republic Day Parade with
Prime Minister, Narendra Modi

Marching alongwith Army Commanders

With former Chief Minister of Uttarakhand Trivenrda Singh Rawat

General Bipin Rawat being honoured by 'Hill Mail'

With National Security Advisor Ajit Doval

Releasing the book 'Hill Warriors'

General Bipin Rawat and Mrs Madhulika Rawat at Golden Temple

General Bipin Rawat with his father and other family members

With wife Madhulika Rawat

Madhulika with daughters Kratika and Tarini

Large family of General Bipin Rawat

Late Mrs Madhulika Rawat with Aaruni Doval, Jyoti Dhasmana, Urmila Singh, Ranjana Bhatt and Chetna Negi

The Warrior on his last journey

Generals and gave them his phone number and told them that he would be available for them 24x7. He also called former General Bipin Chandra Joshi, who had attended his marriage ceremony along with his wife, and insisted on them to attend the Army Day ceremony, his wife was overwhelmed. Later, General Rawat sent a vehicle to escort them for the celebration of 'Army Day'. She felt delighted to attend the function.

General Rawat commending 'Ghatak Platoon' of the Army

General Bipin Rawat always took care of trivial things. This small incident proves that General Rawat, who was a brave soldier for his Army and a merciless Army officer for the enemies, was a person with human values. He was a strict officer, a disciplinarian, despite which he was popular not only among his juniors, but among the Jawans at the lowest rung also. These were unique traits of his character which are hard to find in others, especially among the higher officers. These qualities are everlasting and exemplary for the young officers.

As far as I understood and as I realised during my journalistic relations, he possessed a charm of his own, but his humility, roots to the earth, constant connect with juniors, righteousness and accessibility among the soldiers at the lowest rung, where access to such a higher officer is almost impossible, all these values had their own importance.

Whenever General Rawat could find time, he would love to spend this time among his Jawans. He was always ready for their help. There are innumerable instances of a junior officer or a Jawan being subjected to intimidation by a high-ranking officer. General Rawat would listen to the allegations of the aggrieved and administer justice. He believed in advising with his own examples. Once he had a narrow escape in an aircraft accident in Nagaland, when his helicopter crashed within ten seconds of takeoff, in which he received minor injuries. People thought that General Rawat would take rest for a few days, but without caring for his injuries, he resumed his tour. This incident proved to be a message about bravery and devotion to duty among the Jawans. These virtues made him different from other officers and quite popular among the Jawans.

Devout, Loyal and Righteous

General Rawat was used to keeping the *Srimad Bhagwad Gita*, gifted to him by his father General Lakshman Singh, on the table behind his chair. He viewed it as an inspiration to move forward in life. He lived the life of a soldier inspired by *Gita's* preachings: 'You are entitled to action, never to its fruits.' He had deep faith in God. He had also kept an idol of Tirupati Balaji in his office. Usually, such an idol is not seen in the office of the Army Chief or the CDS. He told me about this idol of Tirupati Balaji, that a *swamiji* along with some priests had brought this idol for him and asked him to instal it in his house. General Rawat replied that most of his time was spent in office. To this, they advised him to instal it in his office. Thereafter, the *swamiji* installed the idol of Tirupati Balaji with proper rituals in his office. General Rawat was truly a devout and righteous Army officer. But this incident also proved that action was as important to him as religion. He preferred the office for installation of the idol instead of his home, which was a temple for his actions.

Honouring Sainya Veerangnayen with UP Chief Minister Yogi Adityanath and the then Uttarakhand Chief Minister Trivendra Singh Rawat

No Corruption, No Malpractice

As Army Chief and CDS, he took several steps to prevent corruption and malpractices in the three Services. As COAS, he court-martialled several officers for unscrupulous deeds. He had adopted the 'zero tolerence' policy for corruption and unethical deeds. He believed that the forces were meant to set ideals before the society. I remembered several officers had gone to court against his decisions. Then he used to say, "We must engage the best lawyer, so that the accused officer gets to pay for his misdeed." General Rawat said that women must be accorded full respect in the Services. Strict action was taken against those who were found guily of exploiting women officers or having affairs with wives of colleagues. Besides expediting settlement of such matters, he stressed on strict action against convicts. Regarding the verdict against adultery by the Supreme Court, under which Adultery Act was abolished by the Supreme Court and declared unconstitutional, Bipin Rawat said that the court may be progressive and unorthodox, but the Services are somewhat conventional. Adopting a firm attitude, he said that permission for such sins would not be permitted in the Services.

General Bipin Rawat had directed all the Army Commanders not to tolerate corruption at any level. Corruption must be stopped at all levels in units of commands. Curbing the corruption in the Services is essentially important and respect for women must be given top priority. He had strictly instructed complete investigation and early verdict on pending issues related to abuse of women. He had clearly instructed that in meetings of higher officers, transparency and zero tolerance for corruption should be promoted at every level. Besides these, he also directed the officers to maintain direct dialogue with Jawans and resolve their everyday difficulties promptly. General Rawat had also released his Whatsapp number with a view to increase direct dialogue with the Jawans. This number was flooded with messages.

General Bipin Rawat with Ram Nath Kovind, former President of India

In fact, General Rawat never tried to conceal the incidents of corruption and immoral acts in the services. Due to his frankness, zero tolerance towards dishonesty, malpractices or indirect corruption, his habit of spontaneous reaction and taking effective action, he had to face the displeasure of officers whose ego and personal benefits received a hit for his conduct. He was also strict on misuse of disability pension. During his tenure, the Services had accepted the government decision to tax disability pension, for which several retired physically challenged officers and Jawans had expressed their dissatisfaction. In fact, General Rawat believed that a number of senior military officers have been misusing this to secure income-tax rebate. He used to ask journalists to publish news about such officers. During his tenure as COAS, the cantonment area was opened for the public. Several Army officers had questioned the decision to allow civilians and general public to pass through the cantonment area. It was a matter of observing distinct individuality from civilians, distinct identity, dignity and pride, but as a believer in inclusiveness, General Rawat firmly stuck to his decision.

□

4

Master Military Strategist

Master of Successful and Right Planning

CDS Bipin Rawat was not only an Army officer holding the highest post and bestowed with the highest numbers of decorations and a fearless soldier, but was a fine military strategist and highly capable defence expert with deep knowledge and vast insight.

During my long career in covering the defence beat, I realised that military strategies chalked out by him were not only effective in the battlefield or battlefront, but these had far-reaching effects on the military and its associated organisations. Why were the strategies of CDS Bipin Rawat so foolproof, firm, accurate, practical and successful? There may be several reasons, but the most important thing, I realised during my coverage of the defence beat and meetings and proximity with him, was his study of the issues. This study was not restricted to books and it was not merely bookish knowledge, but he was fond of reading. He used to continuously observe, study and analyse the society, people and their state of mind, situations, circumstances, occasions, atmosphere, conduct and global perspectives. He used to meet not only the senior officers, but mingle with the soldiers of lower ranks, defence employees and he had even deep reach in the civilians outside military. He used to meet people drawn from different sections, whether they were from Kashmir or from the north-east, from Delhi or any other part of India. That was the reason that he had complete understanding and knowledge about Army and also about different subjects. Analysis of such information, understanding and knowledge were reflected in his well-drawn strategies. He was in favour of indigenisation, modernisation and practical reforms in the military. He strongly advocated for them, as he was a visionary and could visualise the future of military.

General Rawat with Lt General Anil Bhatt and other senior officers

He had visualised the future of the military and also knew where and how any war would be fought. He wanted to prepare the Indian Armed Forces for that war and his strategies were drawn with this aim in mind. During my defence reporting, I observed his work, his modus operandi, working style and his behaviour with juniors and seniors and analysed his strategies, but it was also important to know about the experience of those who were with him during his work or those who were with him during his time away from official life. Lt Gen Rakesh, who worked with Bipin Rawat in the Gorkha unit, was also a family friend. Lt Gen Anil Bhatt also had the good fortune of working with him on many occasions, particularly when General Bipin Rawat was Army Chief. He had worked with him as 15 Corps Commander and later as his Military Secretary.

Lt Gen Rakesh Sharma (retired), who had been witness to very important moments during his tenure and social life, says, "In military operations which include surgical strike, mobilisations or important tactical operations, accurate strategy and plans always proved effective. He was a master in chalking out superb plans with visionary thinking. This was known in the Army and the regiment, but only a few from outside were aware how far Bipin Rawat's ideas and plans were behind any successful military campaign. Apart from being the head of the Army, he was the brain behind many such successful operations."

In fact, Bipin has left behind an exhaustive list of incomplete tasks, apart from an image and imprint of a multifaceted military officer. He was not only drawing up plans and strategies for attacks and fights in a war, but also for positive reforms in the military and making it capable, competent and modern, which resulted in many strategies and campaigns to make the military indigenised and self-reliant. These plans, campaigns, policies and strategies could help in transformation of the Services. Undeterred by the opposition, he had a clear idea about the conduct of Services. Lt Gen Rakesh Sharma opines, "With his sad demise, India has lost a great patriot, a dedicated soldier, a visionary military strategist, who has left behind a great void. To tell the truth, leaving all of us behind, General Bipin Rawat set off on a journey to the other world. If we can make his dreams come true, it would be a true tribute to him."

Self-confident General

About a month before his unfortunate and sad demise, Bipin Rawat had said with all seriousness and responsibility, "India had been facing its biggest threat from China and it was more serious than that from Pakistan." Apart from this, in a reply to a media querry, he said, "For India, China is Enemy Number 1." In this age of soft diplomacy, it was only Bipin Rawat who had the guts to speak candidly in order to tackle China militarily. It was not that his self-confidence was revealed on reaching the topmost post in the military, but this virtue was evident throughout his career. His colleague Rakesh Sharma tells, "As a young officer, without getting distracted at the sharp opposition on a matter, he would say with full self-confidence, 'Excuse me, I do not agree with you on this matter.' With this, he used to dismiss the matter. He used to put his resistance with such humility and self-confidence that most of the matters were resolved without much argument. With his signature smile and persuasive style, Bipin would easily resolve the matter and turn the opposition in his favour and would often neutralise it for good."

General Rawat at a local programme in Srinagar

General Rawat on Kashmir tour with 15 Corps Commander Lt Gen Anil Bhatt

A few months before Bipin got commissioned in 5/11 Gorkha Rifles (BOGRA), people were sure that he would be joining this great unit. Bipin Rawat's father, Lt Gen (then Brigadier) Lakshman Singh Rawat had commanded this unit of 5/11 Gorkha Rifles at Dharamshala and Dabong with full capability. Lakshman Singh Rawat was known for his humility. He used to stress on intense training. Bipin had been awarded with 'Sword of Honour', which was a great achievement and a heartening piece of news. This achievement demanded celebration. His colleagues prepared a well-planned mischievous welcome for him. Captain Ummed Thapa played the role of an assistant and he meddled with Bipin's identity card and Captain Utpal Roy posed as the medical officer. Captain Rakesh Sharma acted as the Adjutant (all of them were Second Lieutenants at that time). Lt Col Madan Gopal successfuly played the role of Commanding Officer. Thus, he was welcomed in the unit in an interesting way. After enjoying the joyous moments, he had the last laugh at the people who were laughing at him and said that he had PCK (in colloquial language it means 'prior information') about this. He knew all, but he was allowing them an opportunity to laugh at him. Sometimes, his colleagues thought that he was telling a lie, but Bipin had great skill which he used to render people speechless, making them agree with him and emerge victorious. Bipin's conduct and his arguments would decisively conclude the matter in his favour.

Unique Personality

Bipin never used his father's authority to throw weight over others even when the latter was commanding the 19 Infantry Division, nor did he ever take advantage of the fact that most of the senior officers of the infantry had been his 'uncles' and their wives his 'aunties' at some time. Neither was he lured by his friends and colleagues in the unit to seek a favour from any 'uncle'. In the unit, he was one among others. He always kept distance from his seniors and maintained friendly relations with his juniors.

Like the majority of Gorkhas, Bipin was very fond of dancing and he would always join the chorus for the song '*Nakkali lai bhagai jhilke le*'. Recounting a related incident, he said, "In Bhatwari (Uttarakhand district), where the unit was conducting training, trainees used to dance the night away and present themselves the next morning for training. Bipin always was in his element in this unit which was famous for rum-lovers. However, Bipin was a gourmet and this many discovered during his postings at Amritsar and Dehradun. In later years, he became moderate in diet for obvious reasons. He was a frugal eater, but during those 40 years, he remained with a sweet tooth. It appeared that the word 'dessert-lover' was coined for him. Once, he devoured one kilo of *motichoor laddoos* (sweetmeat) in one sitting." All agree that Bipin was a cheerful person, ever smiling, always polite and dignified. He was a versatile officer but from time to time, he used to take to seclusion and keep aloof though during rest of the days, he was a cheerful person. Confirming this trait of him, his companion Rakesh Sharma says, "When he was posted as Adjutant at Bhatwari-Harsil, he had information about everything. Nothing used to escape his eyes. In those days, Bipin Rawat, unshaven for weeks, could be seen patrolling on high-altitude hilly areas, which used to be amusing for the onlookers."

When we talk about Bipin, then we must also say a few words about his devout aspect. In the early days of his service, his religious spirit could be seen during his travels to Gangotri and at the annual Durga Puja celebrations in the regiment. During his entire service period, Bipin would go on foot to pay his obeisance at Vaishno Devi temple near Jammu. Installing the idol of Tirupati Balaji in his office and going for *darshan* to Vaishno Devi temple after taking over as Chief of Defence Staff prove his religiosity.

Bipin—A True Professional

According to the officers who had worked with him during his early days of service, Bipin, as a young officer, was a fine blend of perseverance and diligence, professional capability and intellect, self-confidence and wisdom and there were several remarkable and leading examples of this. He was also always filled with elation and joy of life. He never feared the consequences of his views expressed in clear and simple words. All these qualities made him a popular leader. With friends, he was an elated and joyous person and his friends also used to be enthused by his energetic zeal. He inevitably concentrated with clarity and intent on his career and aims. This was the reason for his keeping update on everything; thus he successfully followed the instructions received.

The fact is that Bipin was always the man that he wanted to be. During the first decade of his service, his professtional identity was quite clear. He conducted thorough research before submitting his presentation, whether it was about the Sino-Indian war or China or Uttarakhand vegetation and animal life in Joshimath. He had full control over whatever he said or did. During the last years of the 70s, he was in Amritsar, while in the early 80s, he was in the Harsil sector (Uttarakhand) as a young officer and as an instructor at IMA, Dehradun. No matter where he was posted, he held a post of responsibility and importance. Bipin was destined to reach higher posts. After Defence Service Staff College, Bipin was posted at the Directorate of Military Operations. Clarity and precision in his thinking, instant understanding of matters, ability to prepare the draft after fully understanding the facts and mastery over language were incomparable.

Ever ready on all fronts

Bipin's fate was tied with Dagger Division-19 Infantry Division. First, Lt Gen Lakshman Singh Rawat had commanded undivided 19 Infantry Division from the high Himalyan range to Pir Panjal mountain range. That was the time when Bipin was a young officer posted in the Kashmir Valley. Later, during the early 90s, he had to command his company, which had its unit in the Uri sector. His colleague, Lt Gen (retired) Rakesh Sharma reminisces, "The situation had worsened. Bipin was also entrusted with the task of planning the wargame for the formation by General Officer Commanding (GOC) and this he considered as a great opportunity to learn. Later, he took the command of Sector Rashtriya Rifles, which included Sopore also in its jurisdiction. In due course, he was appointed General Officer Commanding of Dagger Division. Commanding the company, apart from planning operations with the then officers late into the night, reviewing the situation, listening to various and different opinions, there were deep discussions on phone and idle talks also."

Bipin Rawat had cordial relations with his colleagues and peers, but at times he turned furious and clearly displayed his displeasure. Rakesh Sharma knew, "Expressing his anger with one eye half-closed used to be sometimes well planned. This displeasure would act to enthuse the Jawans to finish their work." Sharing his experience, he says, "Many a time, uncomfortable situations would develop due to seizure of IED or explosives and continued attempts at infiltration. Under such situations, everyone had to remain alert. He was to take command of the command post, which was the last post on the road leading from Uri to Muzaffarabad. The Pakistani Army used to engage in incessant firing, particular in the nights on this post. Bipin was a highly inspirational officer, continuously searching for measures to thwart Pakistani firing with snipers, selecting alternate postions and using high-calibre weapons. There was mobility and high morale in the company and always it was Bipin, who was behind it."

Fond of Studies

When he was in Uri, during his service period, Bipin was selected for Command and General Staff Officer course in Germany, for which he had to undertake a language course at Pachmarhi, which he concluded. But, he lost the opportunity to take the Germany course and later, he was nominated for Command and General Staff College in America. His performance at Command and General Staff College, Fort

Leavenworth was so excellent that the institution included General Bipin Rawat in the International Hall of Fame of its alma mater on 4 April, 2022. Bipin always had an inclination towards education and authored several articles on 'national security' and 'leadership' and which were published in various newspapers and magazines. He did M. Phil. in Defence Studies from Madras University and completed his research on 'Military Media War Study' and also secured the Doctorate of Philosophy (PhD) in 2011.

With colleague from Gorkha Regiment Lt Gen Rakesh Sharma

Bipin emerged as a highly professional officer, as Second-in-Command of 5/11 Gorkha Rifles under his close friend Col (later Lt Gen) Rakesh Sharma, and later as Commanding Officer in Kibithu (Arunachal Pradesh). In a number of professional meetings and presentations, he left his contemporary colleagues far behind. It was his first posting in Arunachal Pradesh and later he took the command of this Corps. Subsequently from here, he conducted the memorable Myanmar surgical strike.

General Rawat—Ever aiming at the target

Lt Gen Rakesh Sharma, family friend of CDS Bipin Rawat, says, "Bipin's research was perfect and his self-confidence incomparable. He was a perfect professional. Even today his memories bring tears to the eyes. He never had negative thinking as he was destined to effect changes and get these implemented. 5/11 Gorkha Regiment was celebrating the Golden Jubilee of its Battle Honour Day in Delhi on 4 December, 2021, where it was his last appearance. It was the old Bipin of 1978, who had joined the unit like a whiff of fresh wind. There was a clever brain behind that restlessness, which had reflected upon matters, informed colleagues and friends about that and expressed his opinions! "Dear friend! Wherever you are, be happy and pleased; effect such changes in this world also, that you were trying to effect in the lives here."

A Down-to-Earth General

Remembering General Rawat's cremation, Lt Gen Anil Bhatt, who had worked with General Rawat on a number of occasions, said, "It was a cold afternoon and standing at Brar Square of Delhi Cantonment, I was preparing myself for paying tribute to the worthy son of India. I was thinking, how to offer my final salute to the great military commander, CDS General Bipin Rawat, whom I had the privilege of working with as DGMO, 15 Corps Commander and later Military Secretary. A number of postings in the Army provided me the opportunity to see him as Army Chief and later as CDS. I am proud to have closeness with such a down-to-earth and highly able defence strategist, a profesional soldier."

After preliminary education at Saint and Monk in Shimla and Cambrian Hall in Dehradun, he joined NDA, Khadakwasla in Pune, where, among other fields, he excelled as a highly competent boxer. On being declared best cadet at IMA in December 1978, he was awarded with 'Sword of Honour'. Thereafter, he was given commission in his father's regiment, 5/11 Gorkha Rifles. His father Lt Gen Lakshman Singh Rawat had been the commander of this unit and retired from the Indian Army in the rank of Lieutenant General. Young Bipin Rawat had simultaneously qualified for NDA and pre-medical at the time when his father was commanding a brigade in Dharamshala in Himachal. Was Bipin Rawat in two minds about choosing a career in military or medical? No. His maternal uncle, Col Parmar had said once, "His intention and aim were quite clear—that he had to follow the footsteps of his father for joining the respectable profession of the Army."

Remembering the initial years, Lt Gen Bhatt says, "In the initial years of my service, I knew about General Rawat through his Army reputation among his colleagues and juniors. In fact, I was well aquainted with his younger brother Col Vijay Rawat, who was my junior at NDA, Khadakwasla. Not only Vijay, his entire family was of calm nature and highly reputed. Most appreciable thing about both the brothers was that they entered the Army at a junior level, but they never inspired awe at their being the sons of a very senior military officer or we can say that they never allowed this to be felt by others. When I met Lt Col Bipin Rawat, he had returned after completing a course in Command and General Staff College, US (this course was taken by the topper of the batch), whereas I had returned from UK Staff College. I was very much impressed by his frankness, tactfulness and ever-smiling face. Later, I continued to be in contact with him in the 'power corridor', i.e. in South Block of Delhi and continued meeting him at other places also. After that, whenever I met him, I learned one thing or other during such meetings. Not only was he tactful, experienced and well-informed, he was also a highly dedicated professional. As a junior officer in his entire military career and later as CO and Brigade Commander, he excelled in his work-field and discharged his duties efficiently." Lt Gen Bhatt tells that he took command at Kibithu in Arunachal Pradesh on LAC and in the sensitive area of Sopore in RR sector of Kashmir. As commander of 5 Sector in Kashmir, he successfully controlled the situation and achieved remarkable results in a difficult situation. As a Brigadier, he was selected as commander of the Indian brigade in the UN forces at Goma. His performance there in challenging circumstances was commendable."

Impartial and Popular Bipin

As General Officer Commanding of 19 Infantry Division, he displayed a different aspect of modus operandi on the post. He remained in the Valley for several years at different times and posts. On analysing his work in the Valley, it would be realised that he was acquainted with people from different sections and areas. He used to remain in contact with the Kashmiris and during his tours, he would listen and try to understand their problems, arguments and matters. He would analyse such information, details and input with proper insight and with a flexible approach, always trying innovative alternatives for resolving issues. Besides Bipin Rawat's amiability and independent thinking, Lt Gen Anil Bhatt was very impressed by his quality of accepting any person or any idea without any bias. He remembers, "When Bipin Rawat took over as Army Chief in December 2016, I had the fortune of becoming the Director General of Military Operations. Thereafter, my professional and personal relations strengthened for two reasons—both of us were Gorkha officers and we belonged to the same hilly *devbhoomi* (abode of gods), but, in spite of these two facts, he never deflected from his duties, never differentiated with others on this basis; for him, all were equal." It is believed that General Rawat was selected as Army Chief by superseding two seniors. People could cite different reasons for his selection, but I am confident that the government took a clear decision, taking into consideration his vast commanding experience.

Among children at Army Goodwill School, Pahalgam, J&K

The decision was proved right. "It is true that he had a clear opinion about Army's strategic reaction on the western border with Pakistan. He believed that 'strict penal action' was required on Line of Control to control Pakistan's behaviour and effect change in it. It was implemented with full fervour and it resulted in evident change in the opponent's behaviour.

His reactions to activities in the Valley and strict action against criminals accused of spreading violence depended on his real reach among the public of the area, understanding of the situation and justification of conclusions."

General Rawat—The Breathing Uniform

During the Doklam crisis in 2017, China was trying to build a road for Jhamperi Ridge. It would have been a direct threat to the Siliguri corridor. Lt Gen Anil Bhatt remembers well, "I found him to be a military officer of bold and decisive leadership. That was different reaction against our northern neighbour China and it created a new dimension and course. It was also a fact that his decision to block the Chinese was fully supported by the highest political authorites, underlining their faith in his military capabilities. During those 73 days of crisis, I found him under pressure, but composed and balanced and he became more and more composed and enriched with experience."

General Rawat was very clear in operation, supplies and human management. He said that the Army has to give up the old techniques and be ready to face new challenges. His exemplary individual integrity and his disdain for displaying splendour and ostentation had caused concern among the offenders. He displayed zero tolerance against corruption and unethical military conduct and never pardoned such acts. He possessed all the virtues of an excellent military commander. He was a determined, courageous, brave, daredevil and truthful military officer. He did everything with complete self-confident. He was a soldier who was always in a breathing uniform.

General Rawat's urge to reach out to the junior-most soldiers and employees could be witnessed when neglecting important personal matters; on busy weekends he would head out to meet the Jawans. On Saturdays and Sundays, he would visit the distant areas in the north-east—northern and western border areas to meet junior soldiers and officers. With the resulting information, knowledge and understanding, he would come to appropriate decisions about military operations and guidance. Having worked with him, Lt Gen Anil Bhatt remembers his greatness, "When I was working as Director General Military Operations and 15 Corps Commander in Srinagar, I was filled with complete self-confidence in taking decisions in difficult times, as I had the support of a boss who was always by my side while taking all kinds of risks or facing difficult situations."

Overcoming Challenges without Delay

The fact is that General Bipin Rawat was selected first Chief of Defence Staff because he had fulfilled all the requirements of his earlier challenging posts. He had the capability, vision and passion to become first CDS. He believed that all three Services had to work in a unified manner to justify their roles in the security of the nation. During his brief service period as the Chief of Defence Staff, General Bipin Rawat did remarkable work in the fields of unification of Armed Forces, institution of a unified 'Theatre Command', making the Armed Forces self-reliant and their indigenisation and modernisation. During conversation, Lt Gen Anil Bhatt shares an intimate detail, "Once, one of his batchmates had mentioned about his being a notable boxer in NDA. In many ways, his acts as a military commander were, in fact, like that of a boxer—agility of feet, intentness and quiet aggressiveness at the right moment and ever alertness to protect oneself from the opponent's strike. Like an expert boxer, General Rawat knew how to knock out the opponent at the appropriate moment. Whenever he got a chance, he was prepared to knock out the opponent. His modus operandi was somewhat different from that of others. It had a style of its own. He considered it important to understand what a soldier needed. He prepared us to reach out to the last person or defence personnel in the Army and understand the nuances of every matter. He would listen to your advice, even if it was against his ideas. He was always open to responsible and good advice. He was one of those seniors, whom you viewed from this angle."

During defence reporting, I couldn't find such officers or soldiers, who opposed the view that CDS General Rawat's efficiency and knowledge of military strategy was exceptional. Yes, there was a difference of opinion about some of his non-military decisions and statements, but those were public.

□

5

Inspiration for Youth

Ideal of the New Generation

Perhaps, Bipin Rawat was the first Army Chief with the widest connect with youth. He will always be remembered as an Army Chief responsible for inculcating love for the country among the youth.

One thing he often told me or would say on almost at informal meetings was that military was not a service. Those who consider it as a job or its work as a service, they ought to seek some other job and not join the military. Only those should join the military who were prepared to sacrifice their lives for the country. It was due to his passion for sacrifice for the country that for him, home, family and relatives had become secondary.

General Rawat's talks were practical and inspirational. Usually the doctrines and advice with which he reached out to the youth were always very innovative, unique, useful for life and interesting. Whenever he was among students, he not only advised them, but also listened to them. Along with his arguments, he supported those with examples from life. He didn't like bookish knowledge or speech game; maybe that is why he was a popular and an inspiring General for youth. Wherever he went, he always tried to talk to them and boost their morale. On several occasions, I have seen youth vying for taking selfie with him and he never disappointed anybody. Though he was short on time, he managed to squeeze time for the youth.

It was 10 November, 2018, when CDS Bipin Rawat visited Ludhiana to participate in a programme organised by the Nehru Yuva Kendra. Addressing the youth, he said that they must take to sky rocketing, if they wanted to fulfil their aims. "With sky rocketing, we can at least reach the moon and stars." He used to say that the youth get disheartened if they fail to achieve their aim, but youth should not lose heart. Giving up after facing defeat is not their forte. Youth should be filled with energy and optimism and not accept defeat or feel dejected. Having failed once, they must gear up to attempt again with full energy to achieve their aim. In their second attempt, they should remove their earlier shortcomings. For this, they should not hesitate to seek help from their guides. In a similar programme and in the presence of a large number of youth, he expressed his strong belief that failure inspires a man to success.

CDS Rawat was a supporter of the ancient tradition of *guru-shishya* (teacher-disciple) in Indian schools. He had emphatically called it the basis of our education. Teachers and students could not be indifferent to this. He said at a programme in 2019, "At the training centre, trainers or instructors hammer into young trainees, aspiring for deployment in the military, the resolve to follow the Army ideology that they are taught and always keep this in mind during their career." He said that so long as the Jawans of the Indian Army followed certain five words, the enemy could not harm us.

With his uncle Bharat Singh Rawat and his family in village Saina

The five words were—*naam, namak, nishan, wafadari* and *izzat*. He had explained, "These five words are the basic elements for a soldier, on which his foundation is laid. These are so deeply drilled into his mind that whenever he has to perform his duties, he proceeds ahead without distraction from his duty and keeping in mind these five ethos and assessing his duties on these five touchstones. I am fully confident that so long as the soldiers of India religiously followed these five ethos, the enemy would be routed if it were to cast its evil glance at the Indian Army."

Besides the youth, General Rawat was also quite popular among the Jawans. A strict disciplinarian and a stiff officer, Bipin Rawat was like Yama (God of Death) for his enemies. He was very strict, but for the Jawans he had a soft corner; may be he was the only officer with such a connect with the Jawans. He was always available to help his Jawans. It is said that once he saved the job of a Jawan. A former Adjutant General (Lt Gen Ashwini Kumar) has shared this incident in one of his articles. A Jawan had complained to him that due to his addiction to liquor, he had been put in F-5 category and a termination order had been issued. His argument was that if for the same fault, an officer had been sent to the de-addiction centre, then why was he being discriminated against? Was it because he was an ordinary soldier? On hearing his arguments, General Bipin Rawat got his termination order cancelled.

With his young officers at the Jammu & Kashmir border

CDS Bipin Rawat had given a grand gift to the youth of Uttarakhand, who were desirous of serving the nation by joining the Army. Relaxing the strict criterion for recruitment to the Army, CDS Rawat had fulfiled the dream of thousands of young men to wear the Army uniform. He permitted relaxation to the higher criterion of recruitment in the Army. Considering the fact that due to geographical conditions, the youth from hilly areas are often or on an average shorter in height in comparion to the youth coming from other parts of the country, the youth from hilly areas were given relaxation of 5 cms. in height and the credit for this goes to him.

Born in Pauri district, CDS Rawat had special attachment to Uttarakhand. He always kept a sharp eye on activities on the Indo-China border. He also visited Uttarakhand to participate in the ninth convocation programme of Garhwal University on 1 December, 2020. He visited Dehradun for the last time on 'Uttarakhand Foundation Day' on 9 December, 2021. Whenever he could snatch time from his busy schedule and challenging responsibilities, he would visit Uttarakhand. He visited his village after many years and went to the hilly village of his maternal grandfather also. Wherever he went, he always met the local youth, inspired them and encouraged them to choose a career in the Army.

In short meetings too, he would impress upon them their love for the country and patriotism, which they should never forget lifelong. I feel the energetic youth were his inspiration. He used to see the future of India in them and perhaps, he realised that these youth and students would carry over his new ideas. In fact, Bipin Rawat was an inspirational icon and a beloved General.

□

6

Thus Spake the Warrior!

Enlightenment

Bipin Rawat carried the image of a brave and expert strategist while possessing an equal ability in writing and oratory. His statements alongwith his thought-provoking, significant speeches in an interesting style were examples of his versatility.

Focus on Education and Health

General Bipin Rawat was all for education as the springboard towards resolution of most of the problems. This was evident while he joined a gathering of people aiming to find solutions to the problems plaguing Uttarakhand. Every word which he spoke there reflected his desire to make the state even better, "Formation of Uttarakhand has completed 17 years. Seventeen years is not a long period for a state, but if we think about the happenings in Uttarakhand, then I may say that there has certainly been development in Uttarakhand, but is this development based on proper thinking and with proper ideology and in the right direction? All of us, gathered in Raibar, need to think over it. My father was born in Saina village. I would like to inform those who are unaware about it, that this village comes under Dadamandi Patti, which is near Jahrikhal. If you do not know this, then I think you may be knowing about Lansdowne. It is about one-and-a-half hours away from Lansdowne. My mother was born in Dhanari village, which is near Uttarkashi.

"My parents migrated from their native village and settled down in Dehradun. Why did they migrate? It was for the sake of education; there were no educational facilities in Dhanari or Saina. My father received his preliminary education in Jahrikhal and from there he shifted to Jalandhar. After initial education in Dehradun, my mother had to go to Delhi for further studies, as there was no good college in Dehradun. So, education and health had been the reasons for migration. We will have to give attention to these essentials and I may remind you that nobody will come from outside to help us in this matter. We are living in *devbhoomi* of Uttarakhand and we will have to find a solution ourselves to these problems.

"I was turning the pages of my album today and trying to find out about my visits to the village. In a childhood photo, we were seen going to the village, riding *kandi* and *dandi*. It meant that we had been regularly visiting our village at the age of four to five years, but when schooling started, we didn't get the opportunity to visit the village. I was educated at Dehradun, but when, in 1978, I joined the Army, perhaps I was destined to return to *devbhoomi*. I was posted in Nelang where I remained from 1981 to 1984. In those days, for reaching Telang, one had to cover the distance between Ganai to Suki on foot, from where a road reached up to Harsil. From there, we had to travel to Gangotri and further. Today Nelang has been connected with road. During these three years, we had been travelling extensively in Uttarakhand. We went to Mana, Dharchula and other places in Uttarakhand, visiting areas of Kumaon and Garhwal and learnt about development that has taken place in these areas, but wherever we went, we found health and education had been neglected.

"We are talking about tourism. Six or seven years back, I was with my friends and all of them decided to go on a tour to

Switzerland. I told them, 'Come to Harsil'. They spent six nights in Harsil. While returning, they said, 'We enjoyed Switzerland in Harsil.' I mean to say that we look towards far-flung areas, but forget that there are areas right under our nose, which we see in foreign countries. We have only to provide facilities there. If we try to provide tents, home-stay facilities in tents and provide people with some comforts, then tourism would blossom here. If we want to introduce tourism to this place, we will have to keep one thing in mind and that is our culture. Our *devbhoomi* has a rich culture.

"We will also keep in mind that our culture is not adversely affected by tourism. We should familiarise the tourists coming over to this place with our culture. Jawans from far-flung areas join the Army. Whether it is Kumaon Regiment or Garhwal Regiment or any other military force, people from this area join the forces in a large number, but after retirement, they head for Dehradun or Roorkee. They forget their villages because there are no health and education facilities in the rural areas. These are very important. You can provide your children education up to Class XII here, but what about further education? Then, they have to go to Dehradun or Delhi for higher education in engineering, medical or any other field; but then, they don't return here.

Talking to media at the 'Raibar' programme organised at Tehri Lake

"If we were to open higher education centres similar to our central centre at Uttarkashi and Chamoli, migration from here can be stopped. There have been problems here due to security reasons. Tourism has not taken roots here and security has been a significant reason for it. We have also imposed restrictions on tourism in view of our military institutions and MHA security institutions in the area. But it is the right time to consider allowing relaxation. We should try to work on this aspect. Roads have been built in far-flung areas. Medical facilities of the Army and medical teams of ITBP have also reached the remote areas. Taking advantage of these facilities, we can open frontier areas for tourists.

With former Chief Minister of Uttarakhand, Trivenrda Singh Rawat at his residence in an event of 'Raibar'

"We have different tourism zones. Tourists come to our hills but they are usually elderly persons who come to temples of *devbhoomi* for *darshan*. Besides, proper facilities for trekking, mountaineering, mountain biking can be provided here. I saw in Bhutan that they have developed mountain biking as a means of tourism. I am sure, as a result of the discussions we have in this Raibar programme, we would be able to find a solution to this issue. We will have to find a solution jointly. In fact, *raibar* means 'Come, find a solution to our problems collectively.' It is time to give attention to the development of our *devbhoomi*.

"We should motivate those who have migrated from here and provide them facilities to invest here. We must continue motivating them. If these attempts bear fruit, then I am sure our *devbhoomi* would prosper, progress and the migrated people would start retuning to their roots. We would have to prepare development plans with due care."

(Army Chief Bipin Rawat's address at 'Raibar 2017')

Honour to Brave Mothers is Paramount

"Along with Chief Minister of Uttar Pradesh, Hon'ble Yogi Adityanathji, Chief Minister of Uttarakhand, Hon'ble Trivendra Singh Rawatji and Cabinet Ministers of the state and all VIPs, there are 30 ladies and brave mothers present among us. Countless young men from Uttarakhand have laid their lives for the security of the country. We can never forget the roles our Uttarakhand soldiers played to thwart the terror activities in Kashmir from 1962 till date.

"I feel happy to see the fast progress of Uttarakhand and as Hon'ble Chief Minister stated, the thing which earlier was considered a means of destruction by us, for example, pine leaves, is being utilised for progress. There are several medicinal herbs, which used to be destroyed earlier by the people. Fast progress is being made in the fields of environment and tourism. I would like to extend my gratitude to Hon'ble Chief Minister and his colleagues for providing employment to our youth.

"I emphatically say that the natives of Uttarakhand or who belong to this state would agree that 'if there is paradise, it is here'. As such, we have to take our Uttarakhand properly on the path of progress. We, in the Indian Army, are working relentlessly with Chief Minister's office for the progress of the state. Recently, we have provided facilities in the areas adjacent to the Chinese border for cultivation of walnuts and pine nuts and we are constructing roads. Wherever we have to provide connectivity of any kind, whether it is road, rail or air connectivity, we would work in complete co-ordination with the state government.

General Rawat at an Uttarakhand programme

"I am pleased to inform you that Indian soldiers, brave women and brave mothers have always been honoured in all the programmes organised in Uttarakhand. As such, I feel proud to be a part of this esteemed gathering. Today also, we are witnessing the Chief Ministers of Uttar Pradesh and Uttarakhand honouring the brave mothers. No other honour can be bigger than this for us.

"Uttarakhand has been deploying brave soldiers in the Indian Army. I am confident that Jawans from Uttarakhand would not take their steps back, would confront the enemy and terrorism boldly, even if they have to lay down their lives. Youth and women never withdraw in the face of the enemy. We are proud of you. I don't say that soldiers from other states are not doing their job properly; they too are true to their duties, but the way Uttarakhand has provided brave soldiers to the Army, is incomparable. Thanks for inviting us to this programme and honouring our soldiers. Jai Hind, Jai Bharat, Jai Uttarakhand!"

(Address of General Bipin Rawat in 'Raibar 2019')

CDS General Bipin Rawat said, "Military police mark just a beginning; more participation of women in the years to come."

At a webinar by *Hill-Mail*, CDS Bipin Rawat said, "Strengths and weaknesses of women and men are different. With this in view, if we strike coordination between woman-power and man-power, then there would emerge a power which would be stronger.

"Women must get the chance to join below the officer grade in the Army. Corps of military police are just a beginning; participation of women in the forces will further increase in the times to come. With the contribution of women and men in the Army, the power of the Army would increase. We can't view women with double standards. We are happy about permanent commission."

CDS General Rawat added, "Women and men have different strengths and weaknesses. If we co-ordinate between these different strengths, then the emerging strength would increase the power. We have seen that women possess such power, that is absent in men. Women are serious towards their job and once engaged in it, they don't allow their minds to distract. These days, we notice the need to prepare for cyber and artificial intelligence and women's contribution in all these areas would be important. Whatever work we undertake, women are required to work with men. If women are not with us, we will have to borrow them from the police or civil areas, which would lead to delay.

"Woman power has been very significant in Uttarakhand. Today we know about Bachhendri Pal, Basanti Devi and other such women, but I am going to tell you about a woman who played an important role in unifiying Uttarakhand. We know that there have been great women, like Lakshmi Bai, the queen of Jhansi, Jijabai, Queen Gaidinliu in Nagaland, who earned fame in the country. We, in Uttarakhand, also have our Lakshmi Bai, who is known by the name of 'Teelu Rauteli'. She and her family made crucial efforts to unify Uttarakhand. I am telling you about the lady who existed many years ago. Family of Teelu Rauteli belonged to Uttarakhand. Bhoop Singh was her father and her mother was Maheshwari. She had two younger brothers. A battle was fought in those days on behalf of the Arabs and many parts of India were occupied by force. Under such circumstances, her family raised an Army and thwarted the attempts of Arabs to take Uttarakhand under their control. A folk-song in the name of Teelu Rauteli is in vogue—*'धका धैं धैं तीलू, हे तीलू रौतेली धका धैं धैं।'* When she was 15 years old, she was bethrothed. In those days, Uttarakhand was under attack and her two brothers were wounded in the battle and later they succumbed to their wounds. Meanwhile, Tilu's fiancé also died. After that, she never thought about marriage again.

He explained, "There used to be a Kauthig fair. Teelu wished to attend the fair, but her mother said, 'Forget about going to the fair; you should avenge the death of your brothers and fiancé. If you succeed, you would become immortal in the world.' On hearing this, Teelu built a battalion and fought with the Kathiri army for seven years through Khairagarh. In Tikoli Khal, she faced the first encounter and then she occupied Milaubhan, Chakrata, Saraikhet and many other areas by thwarting the invasion of Uttarakhand by the Arabs. She had a black mare. Arabs had set up camps around Chakrata. The battle had been continuing for seven years. During that period, she was treacherously attacked and she was martyred at the age of merely 22 years. She got her name inscribed in the history of Uttarakhand at a young age. We must know about such woman-warriors. Teelu Rauteli is not the only one, but there are many such great warriors."

□

7

Strong Nationalism, Blatant Dispute

Bipin—Between Opinion and Dispute

Often Bipin Rawat had to face criticism contrary to voices of praise. A strong nationalist has to pay the price for his blunt statements with incessant disputes and harsh criticism.

In December 2018, when his appointment as Army Chief was announced after superseding two senior-most Army officers, then it was said that it was bound to happen. It was clear from the statements of Bipin Rawat that he was seeking the post of COAS and was trying to impress the Prime Minister. Some of his recent statements were considered as his efforts to please the PM with an eye on the post of Army Chief and a higher post after superannuation. The government's decision to appoint him as COAS would be considered impartial and Bipin Rawat was given the responsibility considering his ability, but his critics proved right, when the government appointed Bipin Rawat on these posts, superseding the seniority. The critics were also proved right that he had succeeded in his efforts and become personal choice of the government, especially of Prime Minister Narendra Modi. In fact the dispute that erupted in 2016, when he was appointed Army Chief, superseding two senior officers, was deeprooted. With his statements and actions as an Army officer, Bipin Rawat proved that he believed in a particular thinking and ideology and this ideology had become evident even before he became the General. So, when he took charge as Army Chief, he had to face sharp criticism for his alleged affinity with the Bharatiya Janata Party.

In Uttarakhand's Raibar programme, near Tehri lake

Though he always refuted these allegations, it cannot be denied that unlike any other Army Chief, General Bipin Rawat showed affinity for political and ideological objectives of the party in power. What is more, in full military uniform, he publicly met the chief of Rashtriya Swayamsevak Sangh and claimed that nothing was wrong as "respecting elders has been part of our tradition", thereby drawing criticism from many quarters.

Prime Minister Jawaharlal Nehru had emphatically said that military must not interfere in civilian matters. Unlike the Army of Pakistan or Bangladesh or Myanmar, the Indian military has remained distant from politics. That is why Indian Army has never resorted to toppling the elected government in India, as has been witnessed in other countries.

It was alleged that Bipin Rawat clearly gave statements on the political line of the party in power. As such, there was nothing wrong in regarding him close to a Hindu nationalist

Prime Minister, Narendra Modi. Besides foreign policy and geopolitical issues, whatever he spoke on local politics, was considered 'propower line'. Notwithstanding General Rawat's ideological leanings, his remarks on some non-military and civilian matters had often been considered political, but then he was not a person with such political ambition as observed in respect of Army Chiefs of some countries. To judge his statements and his few actions in this light can only be termed as exaggeration. In fact, he was a true nationalist, who believed in a true nationalist ideology in national interest, which was apolitical and not in the interest of any political party.

At the Stage with well-known lyricist Prasoon Joshi

Considering his statements to be similar to the party in power, his critics said that some of his statements were against the 'apolitical' tradition of the Army. On one occasion, he spoke out that a Muslim-majority party like the All India United Democratic Party could pose a danger to national security. Openly supporting the political claims of the party in power, he said that there had been 'organised infiltration of Bangladeshis' in the north-east. Though his statement was in reference to national defence, security and border infiltration, but it was seen with jaundiced eyes. After this statement of his, minority leaders called him a 'spokesman' of the BJP.

Military luminaries and security experts criticised General Rawat for openly making such statements. Former naval chief, Admiral L. Ramdas, said, "The fact is that we are serving the nation, not the political power. It is wrong for anyone in service as military personnel to express his political views, whether he or she is on the top post or on a lower rank." Some were of the view that "such an Army Chief, participating in local politics, would be more suitable for Pakistan than India. It is unseemly for an in-service Army Chief forming alliance with political masters and making such political statements. He must not forget that India is still a democracy and Armed Forces have to work within the democratic system."

When General Rawat criticised those who opposed the new Citizenship Act, human rights activists and Opposition leaders accused General Rawat of violating the oath he had taken. In December, there had been country-wide demonstrations against the revised Citizenship Act. Youth and students and a particular section were particularly agitated at it. Meanwhile, there was a violent agitation by students, when General Rawat made this comment. Addressing a function, he had said that students from various colleges in thousands had resorted to violence under the political leadership, which should not "lead the youth for violence and arson. This is not leadership. Leaders are those, who lead you in the right direction and provide sound advice." This statement was highly criticised. Opposition leaders and retired senior military officers condemned this statement of his. Most of them were of the view that no active Service chief had perhaps ever displayed the desire to intervene in such a sensitive political matter, which had nothing to do with the Services.

Senior Congress leader, P. Chidambaram sharply replied to this statement, "Political leaders would do what is to be done by political parties. General Rawat should not tell us, what to do, as we do not tell Generals how to fight a war."

Congress leader, Adhir Ranjan Chowdhary also tweeted, "Comments of Army Chief on CAA are highly objectionable, immoral and are beyond understanding." Air Vice Marshal Kapil Kak (retired) said, "Armed Forces of India are apolitical. Army Chief must not make such a statement, which is in favour of or against anybody. This is unconstitutional. Are we following Pakistan's path of politicisation of the Army? Such an unpleasant intervention of top military professionals in the matters of democratic agitations is unheard of in the history of India."

CDS Bipin Rawat had a different type of relationship with Kashmir. During his service period, he had spent a considerable time in Kashmir, commanding a Brigade and Division. General Rawat had been regularly visiting Jammu & Kashmir during his tenure and boosting the morale of the soldiers stationed on frontier posts. He is still remembered by many Kashmiris for his civilian services apart from military services and for his conduct. In northern Kashmir, Bipin Rawat spent almost 10 years when he helped many Kashmiris. Even today, locals of this area praise his words and actions. They say that General Rawat always mixed with the locals, listened to their problems and resolved these.

Attending 'Raibar' programme at the residence of the then Chief Minister Trivendra Singh Rawat in Dehradun

These incidents and stories led his critics to say that Bipin Rawat's behaviour towards the common Kashmiri was quite aggressive. But there is no doubt that being a true soldier and patriot, he was particularly aggressive towards those Kashmiris who used to create unrest in the Valley and oppose the Army at the behest of the enemy-country. Bipin Rawat had issued a statement, "Terrorists coming to Kashmir from Pakistan would cross the border on two legs, but would return from here on four shoulders. They will come and we would be sending them under the soil." This was a clear and strong message for the Army to treat such elements mercilessly, as a result of which the Army Jawans, in their over-enthusiasm, unconsciously dealt with citizens in such a way that led to disputes. So, with his success stories in Kashmir, sometimes such incidents also became a subject of discussion. As such, his memories of Kashmir were filled with bitterness of disputes along with sweet-sour remembrances.

In Kashmir, under a well-thought strategy to create unrest, masters across the border were sending their agents to instigate stone pelting. Suddenly, stone pelters in

Kashmir would appear at a place and start pelting stones at the Army, creating an uncomfortable situation for the Army. General Bipin Rawat made a statement on stone pelters in 2017, which created ripples. He had said, "How I wish these stone pelters would operate weapons instead of pelting stones at us! I would be happy then." It was inferred from his statement that the Army would be at liberty to fire at the demonstrators. He had said, "People are pelting stones at us; they are throwing petrol bombs at us. If my Jawans ask me about their course of action, then what should I say? Stop and die! I would come with a national flag and an attractive coffin and would send your body with full respect to your home? Should I tell them like this as a chief? But the right thing that I have to do is to keep up the morale of my soldiers and military officers serving there in such a difficult situation at any cost."

During the year 2017, Major Litul Gogoi, an Army officer was deputed on behalf of 53 Rifles in Srinagar. During the Lok Sabha by-elections scheduled to be held on 9 April, the officer used a young Kashmiri craftsman, Farooq Ahmed Dar as a shield against the stone pelters.

According to Litul, he took this action to protect electoral staff and Jawans on duty. He caught a young man, who was leading the stone pelters and inciting them and tied him on the bonnet of his jeep and used him as human shield. But, Jammu & Kashmir police narrated the incident in a different way saying that an unarmed embroidery craftsman, Farooq Ahmed Dar was coming out of the polling booth after casting his vote, when he was caught and used as a human shield.

Photos of Dar tied to the moving jeep were published in media, his video was shown on TV. Litul Gogoi had applied defensive strategy to protect his convoy from stone pelters. Besides, ultra-nationalists, who consider Kashmir their own, but all Kashmiris as strangers or terrorists, people of particular section also found this method commendable and brave. All of them saw a hero in Major Litul, praising him for managing a difficult situation without bloody fight. But most of the people did not find this method logical, conforming to human rights, constitutional and lawful. Major Litul Gogoi was criticised for this action and the Army was advised to avoid this extremism in Kashmir, as Kashmir is also an international subject.

Bipin Rawat himself said that use of human shield in such matters is not an accepted method. To protect the serious image of the nation and the Army internationally, protecting this action of Litul Gogoi, General Rawat said, this should be seen as an 'innovation' or 'a new counter method.' Major Gogoi was decorated with 'Chief of Army Staff Condemnation Card' on 22 May, 2017. This commendation card is recommended by the Chief of the Army Staff himself. General Rawat awarded this medal to Litul Gogoi for his efforts in anti-terror operation, which meant this medal is the approval of his act and proved it right. But General Rawat had to face severe criticism for this decision. Now, apart from these criticisms, this criticism is itself under dispute. How far this is right?

In an interview in 2018, in reference to the appointment of Satya Pal Malik, General Rawat said, "We want to allow the new Governor some time." This statement sounded as if he was not talking as an Army officer, but as if he was talking on behalf of the government. In 2017, he had extorted the soldiers, "Enemies must fear you and your own people should also be in awe of you. We are, indeed, a friendly force, but when we are called for maintaining law and order, then citizens of the country, people must fear us." This statement was highly criticised, but in a sense, Bipin Rawat had said nothing wrong.

His viewpoint was right because how can peace be restored, if anti-social elements in the society are not fearful of military action? And how can the Army's importance be established among the public? He was boosting the morale of his soldiers.

With Jawans deployed on the north-east border

His advice about disability pension for the Jawans of Indian Army also created a controversy. In fact, he had warned about those soldiers who were falsely presenting themselves as disabled. He had said, "If any soldier is genuinely disabled, we would particularly consider his case and provide him financial help, but I am warning those who prove themselves disabled through false means so as to earn money." General Rawat was condemned over such a true fact and on enquiry into the matter, it was proved that General Rawat was right as investigations revealed several cases of such irregularities. In fact, Bipin Rawat had believed in 'zero tolerance' policy against corruption, whether it was related to a person, organisation or institution, or it was financial or procedural matters. He had taken strict action against an officer in Lucknow, who had been accused of sending indecent messages and also in a matter of irregularities in a matter related to land.

CDS Bipin Rawat's advice to 'disabled' soldiers created a ruckus and dispute. Similarly for his proposal relating to retired soldiers, General Rawat was fiercely criticised by former officers of the Indian Army. He had proposed a special code of conduct governing retired soldiers. However, Army Headquarters had clarified that it did not support any such code of conduct. Importance of General Rawat's proposal could have been realised in view of uncontrolled proliferation and instability of communication media, like social media, TV. During an interview, replying to a question about the combat role of women in the Army, he had said, "Women may face inconvenience on their deployment as fighters along with men. They could complain about men peeping into the tent, while dressing. They (women) would say that somebody is peeping, so we would have to provide a sheet around them."

With renowned Cricketer and Hon Group Captain of Indian Air Force, Sachin Tendulkar

He was explaining the practicality of challenges of deployment of women in frontier areas. He was talking about normal mentality and habits of men. This quite normal and practical statement of Bipin Rawat also attracted fierce criticism. Attempts were made to paint him as anti-women. Similarly, as Army Chief, he had expressed his views on recruitment of homosexuals in the Indian Army, saying, "Thinking of Indian forces is almost similar to that of conservative Indian society. Military is conservative. We are not modernised nor have we been Westernised." Many considered it regressive thinking or personal experience or thinking of General Rawat.

Bipin Rawat was appointed Joint Commander of all the three Services, but with greater honour to him, there often continued trivial whisperings about him in all the three forces. In one of his statements, Bipin Rawat described the Indian Air Force as a 'helping hand'. The then Chief of IAF, Air Chief Marshal, RKS Bhadoria publicly criticised him, "It appears that calling a prominent organ of the country's defence network and fundamental structure as helping hand weakens the Air Force, proving it to be of inferior status."

General Rawat also commented a number of times on Chinese activities in Nepal. The Chinese Army took serious exception to his remarks naming China as the biggest threat to India. Lack of trust is an obstruction in resolution of border dispute between India and China. There have been 13 rounds of talks between India and China, but due to lack of mutual trust, they have failed to resolve the dispute. China wants 'my way or no way'. It wants acceptance to all its terms. India is firmly facing it. We cannot be pressurised or pushed back. China is quite capable technologically and has resorted to cyber attacks against India. India is also actively engaged in strengthening its cyber defence system to deal with China's cyber attacks. Such statements may nonetheless be welcome, but General Rawat had on many occasions said certain things about neighbouring countries and other international relations, which may have ruffled the feathers of the concerned nations and may be justifiable at his personal level, but statements in conflict with international relations by this high-ranking Army officer can never be justified. But that is a different thing that these statements had been particularly underlined for some reasons.

CDS General Bipin Rawat posed a question during a meeting in Delhi. He asked, "Will China's increasing closeness with Iran, Turkey and Afghanistan not lead to clashes of civilisations again, under which Chinese and Islamic civilisations would unify against the Western world?" The question raised by the CDS was merely an intellectual interpretation. He just presented his assessment and view-point. It was not an official statement of the Army or the government, but the media presented it in such a manner that it sowed seeds of dissent. Next day a meeting of Foreign Minister, S Jaishankar with his Chinese counterpart, Wang Yi was scheduled to be held in Dushambe under 'Shanghai Co-operation Organization'.

Frank discussion on every issue of country's interest

Prior to this meeting, S Jaishankar had to tell his Chinese counterpart, Wang Yi, clarifying, "India has never supported the principle of clashes of civilisations." Everybody said that CDS should evade such public statements, which could have adversely affected India's foreign relations. CDS has not given any official statement in the meeting. He had just raised a hypothetical question before defence strategists and intellectuals! It was the media that blew the matter out of proportion, but Bipin Rawat was trapped in a dispute! He learnt a lesson of avoiding to brighten his image through media. It was advisable for him to be seen and or felt, but not heard. Similarly, when Bipin Rawat said, "When we talk of Jammu & Kashmir, then it also includes PoK, Gilgit and Baltistan. PoK is an illegally-occupied area as it has been illegally occupied by our neighbouring country. This illegally-occupied area is controlled by terrorists, not Pakistan." There was no deficiency in Bipin Rawat's statement, except being a little exaggerated and lesser factual. Home Minister, Amit Shah also had given such a statement, but being a political leader, he can say such things, but an Army officer cannot be so straightforward. The reason for disputes over most of his statements is his forthrightness, sincere narration, non-artificial conduct, speaking out his mind and free thinking.

□

8

A Fiery Life

Highly Dutiful

Generally a warrior lives with his culture and is least concerned with social concerns, but Bipin Rawat was a unique person who was a rare combination of military culture and social culture.

Col Satyapal Singh Parmar is maternal uncle of General Bipin Rawat. Traditionally, he too is the representative of families serving in the Army. He retired as a Colonel in the Army. Col Satyapal Singh Parmar is among one or two persons, besides his mother and father, who spent time with him from his childhood to two days before the fateful accident. Due to some circumstantial and family reasons, Col Parmar had the opportunity to stay close to him. General Bipin Rawat too, not only had high regards for him, but he used to consult him on every family matter and seek his help. After the sudden demise of CDS General Bipin Rawat, memories of Col Parmar are very precious, which provide intimate insight into his life. Although stirring those sad memories does not seem fair, but still I talked to him and he shared his memories with me; some memories that are just associated with him.

Second Lieutenant Bipin Rawat with his maternal grandfather Kishan Singh Parmar and maternal uncle, Col Satyapal Singh Parmar

First News

Taking a deep breath, Col Parmar recalls, "Even today, it is hard to believe that he has left us and he is not with us; now only his memories linger. Madhulika Rawat always accompanied her husband and would go with him wherever she was officially entitled to accompany him." Col Parmar further says, "I was in the bank on that fateful day of 8 December, 2021 when my brother-in-law called me from Nagpur three-four times. I couldn't pick up the phone as I was in the bank, though I did think that there must be some reason for his repeatedly calling me. Was there any emergency? I dialled his number. He said, 'Where are you, brother? Please watch the TV, General Rawat's helicopter has met with an accident.' I couldn't believe the news. Immediately I called Madhulika. I dialled her number four-five times but there was no reply. There was no return call, so I called his staff officer, Col Harendra Singh. I didn't get any reply from him also. Then I phoned General's PA, Baljit Singh. I failed to contact him. I thought it was strange. Then I called my home and said, 'Switch on the TV.' When I returned home, I saw all were weeping while seated before the TV."

According to Col Parmar, his last meeting with CDS Bipin Rawat was on 6 December at his residence. They had gone to their house for lunch. In fact, lunch was just an excuse; they all had gathered at his residence to discuss and finalise the celebration of birthday of his grandson (daughter's son) on 14 December. General Rawat was also meeting his maternal uncle to enquire about the progress of his house under construction in Dehradun, and also about the requirements in that connection.

Committed to the Army

General Bipin Rawat's commitment to duty was of highest standard. He dedicated his whole life to the Army. In fact he was a true nationalist and considered serving the Army as the greatest service to the nation. For his commitment to his responsibilities and his diligence, he was often rebuked by elders in the family. Often he did not accept or smilingly avoided reproach, complains, rebukes by elders for family, dignity, health and other reasons. Col Parmar says that he was always worried about General Rawat's security.

Generally, citizens or civilians carry an opinion about military officers that they lead a life of pleasure and prosperity and they are not made to work harder. They are less busy, but enjoy functions and festivities. On 6 December, when General Bipin Rawat was visited by his maternal uncle, the former was caught in a busy schedule. In spite of it being a holiday, he had three meetings lined up. He promised to take some time off and return by 1.30 in the afternoon. He didn't come. When called, he informed that he had taken some food and would come soon, but not for lunch. Col Parmar tells, "We had been waiting for him since 12 o'clock, but he could come only by 2.30. We had a discussion for only about 20 minutes, when suddenly he got up and said, 'Oh! I forgot, some people are coming to meet me. They might have come,' and leaving the discussion unfinished, he went to the other room." So civilians' concept of Army officers not being as busy as other high officers or leaders is not justifiable.

An Unfinished Meeting

Remembering the last meeting of 6 December, Col Parmar said, "General Rawat consulted me on every family matter. This time the matter was regarding the construction of his house and other family matters. When he was the Southern Army Commander, he wanted to settle down in Noida. Although I agreed to his proposal, I asked him if he would be living in a Noida flat, even after becoming a General. 'You will have to settle in Dehradun to serve Uttarakhand.' His wife also agreed with my advice."

Col Parmar became emotional while remembering General Bipin Rawat and started to talk about his childhood, about which only a few people knew. He said, "General Bipin Rawat was born in the Military Hospital, Dehradun. When he was in his infancy, his face was so soft that just a small pressure by a finger would leave a mark on the face. When Bipin Rawat's parents took him to his maternal grandfather's village for the first time, he was six-months old and they stayed there for three months. His second visit to the village took place when he was posted as Second Lieutenant at Harsil. Thereafter, when he became Army Chief, he went to his maternal grandfather's house and also his native village, Saina in Pauri Garhwal.

General Rawat with his childhood friend and cousin, Brigadier Shivendra Singh

High Values

Col Parmar's was a joint family. He had elder brothers, but they didn't get such an opportunity as Col Parmar got. He had stayed with all the three children of Lt Gen Lakshman Singh Rawat, that is, with his niece and nephews. General Bipin Rawat followed his family traditions and values at every step. It was in his nature to respect his elders, gain from their experience, age and seek their advice and guidance on matters of importance. Confirming this, Col Parmar said, "When General Bipin Rawat was Southern Army Commander, he was looking for a suitable match for his elder daughter Kritika. Suddenly his eyes fell on an advertisement in the newspaper. After reading it, Bipin called me and asked me to come to Pune immediately. I reached Pune and both of us reached Mumbai by road the very next day. We met the family of the boy. They were residing in Mulund. They also visited our house and then Bipin asked me for my opinion. I replied, 'They are good people and theirs appeared to be a noble family. They have their factory in Mulund and they live there.' His daughter was married at his residence, the New Delhi Army House."

About Lt Gen Lakshman Singh Rawat

Undoubtedly, parents play an important role in moulding their children. Lt Gen Lakshman Singh Rawat, father of General Bipin Rawat, was an ideal and heroic personality. But, his mother also played a prominent role in developing his personality, like in shaping his character in early childhood, inculcating values like passionate patriotism, respect for women, etc. Describing his brother-in-law and Bipin Rawat's father, Lt Gen Lakshman Singh Rawat, Col Parmar says, "General Lakshman Singh Rawat was posted at Dehradun. Our sister was also residing at 14 New Road, Dehradun. Negotiations regarding their marriage started and both were married in 1957 at Dehradun. His initial postings were in Lucknow, mostly at IMA, Dehradun and Gorkha Centre. In those days, the centre of Gorkha 11 Regiment was Dehradun. Bipin's childhood was spent in Dehradun and Lucknow. General Rawat had no permanent residence in Dehradun. In those days, when he was posted in field areas, he didn't get any family accommodation. So, the children had to spend a long time at our residence at 14 New Road, Dehradun. When General Lakshman Singh Rawat was posted in Bhutan, then also these three children—Bipin,

Kiran and Vijay stayed with us in Dehradun."

The career profile of Lt Gen Lakshman Singh Rawat was quite impressive. After becoming Lt Gen, he commanded 10 Corps. Bipin Rawat's sister Kiran was married in Bathinda. Thereafter, he was made the Chief of Staff, Southern Command. Marriage of Bipin Rawat took place in Delhi. Madhulika's family had come to Delhi from Shahdol, Madhya Pradesh, whereas Lakshman Singh Rawat's family had come from Bathinda. It was after the marriage of Bipin and his brother Vijay that General Lakshman Singh was posted at Army Headquarters, as Deputy Chief of Army Staff and he retired from that post. He could reach to one of the topmost posts in the Indian Army with his sheer hard work and merit. He was a simple and unassuming person, who loved to help people and was an honest man. All his values were inherited by his son General Bipin Rawat to a great extent.

Bipin Rawat was four years elder to his cousin, Brigadier Shivendra Singh. Both of them spent their childhood together in Dehradun. Later also Brigadier Shivendra Singh spent memorable days with Bipin Rawat. He shared memories of such moments with the author, "The year was 1971. Indo-Pakistan war was being fought. We were quite young in those days and were living in our maternal grandmother's house in Dehradun. Bipin Rawat and his younger brother Vijay Rawat and some cousins were also staying in the house. Meanwhile, we were informed by the Army on 11 December that our father, Col Onkar Singh, deployed at the Chamb-Jaurian front, was martyred in the war. The news stunned all of us and the house was grief-stricken. In the evening, Bipin Rawat came. I was nine-years old and he was around 13. Consoling me, he said, 'All of us would join the Army. Shivendra, we would pay tribute to *mausaji*. We would salute him in the Army. Those who are brave and valiant are destined to such a death. They attain martyrdom. We are proud of our *mausaji* who laid down his life for the country.' It was 11 December, 1971.

"Bipin passed the NDA in 1974, appeared in the SSB merit list, joined Academy and then he came to our house and told Shivendra Singh and his younger brother, 'Look, I have made a beginning towards what I had promised you on 11 December, 1971. You also get started with the preparations. You will also go to NDA at an appropriate time. All of us would join the Army and will be serving in Infantry.' At that time, Bipin Rawat's father was also in the Amry. He was a Colonel in the 5th Battalion of 11th Gorkha Regiment. Bipin Rawat had started setting an example at the tender age of 13 years. He displayed his leadership qualities among his brothers and in his family.

With family friends

"The NDA training is of three years divided into six terms. There is a test in the third term, in which the cadet has to jump into water from a height. If the trainee fails to clear this test, he is demoted to the position of six months back. General Rawat got confused in this test and could not finish the jump. He was backtracked by six months. Immediately therafter, when Bipin Rawat visited Dehradun during the holidays, he joined the IRMCA swimming pool the next day and started practicing every day for three hours. With the holidays finishing when he returned to NDA, this time he offered to jump in the first place. He had cleared the test with his first jump this time.

"When Bipin Rawat was determined in his aim, he would never think about anything else. He would put his heart and soul to achieve his aim. His self-confidence was of the highest order and his passion for hard work and devotion were also unsurpassable. Bipin passed out from IMA with the 'Sword of Honour'. It is rare for a cadet, who has lost six months, to get the 'Sword of Honour' in the next term! It may not be possible in the times to come to emulate such a feat. I think he was the first and last cadet to add this achievement to his name. That was the strength and capability of Bipin Rawat that helped him perform such an act.

"Bipin Rawat was commissioned in his father's 11th Gorkha Rifles 5th Battalion. Meanwhile, his younger brother and Shivendra followed in his footsteps and entered the National Defence Academy. After being attached to the battalion commanded by one's father, a person has to work harder than others because not only has he to meet the standards set by his father, but surpass them also."

Shivendra says about it, "This happened with me also. I had also joined 10 Garhwal Regiment. My father Col Omkar Singh from this unit was martyred in the Chamb-Jaurian battle of 1971. It means that a new Second Lieutenant has to work harder, especially in the regiment where his father had been an officer. He is told 'You are his son'. He has no other option, but to work harder for earning his name and place in the forces, in regiment, and among the Jawans. Bipin Rawat achieved all this within two-and-a-half years. Any course that Bipin Rawat undertook, he came out with flying colours, got top grades and earned a name. Meanwhile, he established such an identity, created such a standing that people started saying, 'Look, he is Lt Bipin Rawat sir, whose father Lakshman Singh Rawat was the earlier CO.' Earlier, they used to say that he is the son of Lakshman Singh Rawat and his name is Bipin Rawat."

Brigadier Shivendra Singh Rawat remembers, "Bipin Rawat always used to be in a mission mode. He had an obsession, a determination to do something good for the country, for the Army and for himself. He wanted to earn fame."

Bipin Rawat worked hard in the field areas where he was posted. He earned his name wherever he was commissioned, or deputed, whether it was the north-east or north. He spent a considerable time in Jammu & Kashmir. During his tenure, he was posted as Commander at a number of places. He was Commander of the 5 Sector Rashtriya Rifles in Sopore, which is considered to be a very dangerous area of Jammu & Kashmir. Before that he had commanded his unit in Arunachal Pradesh, on the India-China border. Bipin Rawat was also posted in the military operation branch. His tenure and experience here was quite different. He went to Congo under the UN Peacekeeping Force as Brigade Commander. The point is that his military experience had been of 360 degrees and was broadbased.

Remembering Bipin Rawat, Brigadier Shivendra Singh says, "When I was Commander in RR 12 Sector of Baramula, he came to IG wing in Sofia, Pulwama after becoming Major General. There was a briefing in Corps Commander's office, where all COs and Commanders were present. There also were four General Officers Commanding (GOCs) and each was expected to give a briefing for at least half an hour. Bipin Rawat was the third person to brief. Earlier the two GOCs had given the briefing and each of them had shown about 50-60 slides during that half an hour, giving a detailed explanation. When it was Bipin Rawat's turn, he merely showed four slides and concluded his presentation within 12-15 minutes. He explained everything in those four slides and in 12-15 minutes. So, this was the clarity, self-confidence and simplicity of his ideas. At tea, after the briefing, I met his staff officer, Col JS. I asked him, 'You had prepared only four slides, whereas the rest showed so many slides.' He replied, 'Sir, these slides were prepared by him only. We were not aware what he had prepared and what not. He prepared these slides himself and briefed himself. In fact, he has a different style of working. He does every task in his own style, in his own manner and mostly without depending on others. This is the reason for clarity in his information and ideas'."

Brig Shivendra narrated another incident regarding Bipin Rawat's commitment towards his work and responsibilities. When he was Corps Commander with 3 Corps Dimapur, Shivendra Singh Rawat was also with him, spending his leave. His father Lakshman Singh Rawat was also present. Bipin Rawat was habitual to meeting and touching his father's feet, if possible and given a chance, before leaving for and returning from some far off place. "One day when he left on a flight, he touched his father's feet as usual. He left and within minutes, his ADC informed that Core Commander's helicopter had crashed." Panic broke out. Immediately a vehicle was called and as he was about to leave, a convoy of vehicles from the guesthouse arrived. The convoy stopped and Bipin Rawat stepped out of a vehicle. Shivendra remembers that his combat dress was torn at some places. He immediately went inside. Shivendra says, "I felt relieved on seeing him. We were quite alarmed at the news of the helicopter crash. I also accompanied Bipin inside. Bipin Rawat went directly to his father, touched his feet and there was a temple nearby, where he went and with folded hands paid obeisance and then went to his room. I asked from outside the room, 'May I come in?' He replied, 'Oh! Yes, yes.' When I entered, I saw that he had removed his shirt. He had received some cuts and bruises. He was bleeding also. Without delay I called for the nursing assistant, who bandaged him. I asked him to go to Arunachal Pradesh the next day or the day after. He said, 'No, I'll go today. I have called for the helicopter.' I tried hard to dissuade him, but he was adamant. Bipin Rawat came out of his room and once again met his father, touched his feet and with folded hands went into the temple before leaving. He was back home the same evening. It is true that Bipin Rawat had unwavering self-confidence and decision-making capabilities. Undoubtedly, Bipin Rawat was a bold and fearless person."

After becoming GOC, Bipin Rawat went to the same house, where his father had once stayed after becoming GOC. Shivendra also had gone to his father's old house after becoming GOC as he had spent his childhood here and now after becoming GOC, Bipin also had gone there. Similarly he was GOC, Mumbai area, where his father also had been posted. Shivendra remembers that Bipin had mentioned about these coincidences when he became the Army Chief. He termed it as Fate and said, "No one can do anything about it." Shivendra was then a brigadier. He recalls that after becoming the Army Chief, he visited General Bipin's office, where he was warmly welcomed. He offered tea and not once made me feel that we had brotherly relations. There, that relation was that of Indian Army's Brigadier and the Army Chief. But, in his office he addressed me affectionately and talked as we used to talk in our childhood." After becoming CDS, whenever Shivendra called on him, General Bipin Rawat never made him feel that he was on such a high post, where nobody in the family had ever reached. He maintained brotherly and friendly relations.

Brigadier Shivendra Singh Rawat recalls another incident about Bipin Rawat. He tells, "When he was Corps Commander, then one day sister-in-law Madhulika Rawat rang me up. She said, 'Shivendra, I'll be visiting Dehradun. There is a marriage ceremony. When I attend the marriage, I would need accommodation and a car. Can I get these facilities?' I replied, 'Why not? You are the wife of a Corps Commander, you will definitely get it.' Then, she put a condition that General Bipin must not know about it. 'If he would get to know of it, he would be annoyed.' I said, 'Won't tell him, *Bhabhiji*.' Anyhow all arrangements were made in Dehradun. But I don't know how Bipin came to know about this arrangement somehow. *Bhabhiji* rang up and sounded nervous. She told me, 'Bipin said, "You are going to attend the marriage which is a personal function, make arrangements for your stay and travelling on your own." No Shivendra, neither I need accommodation nor any vehicle. If he comes to know, it would be a problem'."

As a journalist, I had also realised that Bipin Rawat was a person who didn't want to enjoy the facilities, which were easily available to officers and their families.

Bipin Rawat was a down-to-earth person. Even after reaching the heights of his career and capabilities, he was rooted to earth. It was a great value that he possessed. Brigadier Shivendra Singh Rawat recalls another incident, "A retirement ceremony for the officers is held in Delhi. In 2018, he was Army Chief and I was retiring, so I went to his office. On retirement, Army Chief gives a certificate. When I went to him to obtain the certificate, he said smilingly, 'Had I been retiring as an Army Commander, I would have been standing here with you.' Both of us were to retire on 31 March, as his birthday was on 16 March and mine on 22 March. Just think, he was aware at that time that had he been an Army Commander, both of us would have retired together."

In all my meetings with him, I found that Bipin Rawat was a simple, soft, determined and fearless person with steely self-confidence. He had high capability to work and be self-dependent; he performed every task himself. Not only was there clarity in intent and thinking, he had 360-degree experience about everything. After discharging his duty as Army Chief, he was elevated to become the first CDS and this could have not happened without a reason. He loved children very much but as he remained very busy, he could express his emotions on a few and far between occasions. According to Brigadier Shivendra Singh, "He used to hide his love and emotions even with the family and wouldn't express his feelings."

He was completely devoid of pretence. Outwardly Bipin Rawat was very hard, but he had a soft heart within—a quality which he never displayed. All this was due to the fact that his life was meant for the Army, for India—for him, the country was foremost and family was secondary. Philately was his hobby. There were a number of rare postage stamps in his collection. He loved dogs very much and rearing dogs was his hobby. He was as avid reader; whenever he found time, he would start reading something new.

Brigadier Shivendra Singh Rawat summarised Bipin Rawat's life, saying it was always full of bang. "During the 1971 war, when my father became a martyr, he had boldly announced his decision to join the Army. He joined the Army and passed with a bang, earning the 'Sword of Honour'. When he became Army Chief, it was also with a bang and he superseded some. It was a bang that made him CDS and his leaving the world was also explosive. So, that man was explosive everywhere."

□

9

Tributes to a Great Soul

The fame of the supreme protector of the country's border—CDS Bipin Rawat—had no boundary. Even enemies respected his bravery and courage. Condolence messages that poured in from all corners of the world are proof of this.

I am shocked to hear about the untimely demise of General Bipin Rawat and his wife. The country has lost a valiant son. His

selfless service to the motherland for four decades will always be remembered as exceptional valiance.

—**Ram Nath Kovind,** Former President of India

✣✣✣

General Bipin Rawat served India with complete dedication. He was a true patriot and a valiant warrior. He made important contribution to the modernisation of our Armed Forces and security system. His insight and views on military matters were unique. I am deeply grieved to hear about his demise.

—**Narendra Modi,** Prime Minister

✣✣✣

Chief of Defence Staff, General Bipin Rawat's untimely death is an irreparable loss to the Armed Forces and the nation. General Rawat served the country with exceptional courage and dedication. As first CDS, he chalked out the plan for jointness of our Armed Forces.

—**Rajnath Singh,** Defence Minister of India

✣✣✣

This is a sad day for the country, as we have lost our CDS General Bipin Rawat. He was one of the most valiant soldiers, who served the motherland with complete dedication. His exemplary contribution and dedication is hard to describe in words.

—**Amit Shah,** Home Minister of India

✣✣✣

Army's contribution should be depicted in films

I had met him a few days before and I have been meeting him often. He was concerned about films and would talk about how films can show detailed, positive and inspirational contributions made by the Army. He used to discuss with me about this and when I heard the sad news about him, I could not believe it and am yet to come to terms that he is not among us.

Express love for your country always
I may live or not, this India must live.
Turn my veins into wire and make a sitar *of these,*
Play Bharat raga *on me and tingle wires repeatedly.*
This love for the country should overflow from the eyes.
I may live or not, this India must live.
Crush me, lay me on the paths to fields,
Scatter my dust on the hills, in sand
My identity must be mixed in its soil.
I may live or not, this India must live.
Enemy, remain within your bounds
Learn to tell the truth, my India is immortal.
Let this power of devotion be displayed excessively,
I may live or not, this India must live.
I swear I won't forget you even for a moment
Every drop of blood is yours, yours is offered to you.
This is the honour of war, this pride must remain,
I may live or not, this India must live.

—Prasoon Joshi
Poet, Lyricist and Chairman, Censor Board

❖❖❖

My deep condolences on the death of Indian Chief of Defence Staff, General Rawat and his wife and associates. We would ever remember his exceptional leadership capabilities, who served his country and worked for strengthening US-India relations.

—Antony Blinken
US Secretary of State

❖❖❖

General Rawat has left an indelible imprint on Indo-US defence partnership and he played a pivotal role in transforming the Indian Armed Forces into an organisation of unified war capability.

—Lloyd Austin
US Secretary of Defence

❖❖❖

General Bipin Rawat was a learned man, a valiant soldier, a leader and for me a generous host. We express condolences on the death of General Rawat and others in this terrible accident.

—Alex Ellis
British High Commissioner to India

❖❖❖

India has lost a great patriot and a dedicated leader. Russia has lost one of the closest friends, who played a great role in strengthening our special bilateral and empowered strategic partnership. Goodbye friend! Goodbye, Commander!

—Nikolay Kudashev
Russian Ambassador to India

❖❖❖

We deeply grieve the death of CDS Bipin Rawat, his wife and many defence officers. We would remember CDS Rawat as a great military leader and advocate of France-India defence relations.

—Emanuel Lenin
French Ambassador to India

✤✤✤

The news of the death of CDS Bipin Rawat, his wife and 11 other officers in a helicopter crash is exceedingly painful. It is a great loss to our country. I offer my tearful tribute to these worthy sons of Bharatmata. I join their families in their grief.

—Lata Mangeshkar
Queen of Melody

✤✤✤

General Bipin Rawatji! We, grateful Indians, would remember you for ever. May all deceased souls rest in peace! May flowers of words dedicated to my bravehearts will always remain so.

—Manoj Muntshir
Lyricist

✤✤✤

The country has lost a valiant soldier, a unique Commander, a reformist leader and a visionary soldier in CDS General Rawat. Last salute to the brave son of Bharatmata, General Bipin Rawat and his wife! Respectful last salute to all the fellow travellers of that flight!

—Kumar Vishwas
Poet

✤✤✤

Death of Bharatmata's brave soldier, an experienced and able Army Chief and a man responsible for the modernisation of Indian Armed Forces, CDS General Bipin Rawat and officers of other Armed Forces in a helicopter accident is a great national loss. Nation would always remember their service to the nation.

—Swami Ramdev
Yog Guru

✤✤✤

Goodbye, General Rawat and Madhulika Rawat. May their souls rest in peace! Last few days have been very pathetic and sad. It is hard to believe of his sad demise. Oh God! What has happened?

—Aruni Doval
(wife of Ajit Doval)

✤✤✤

I am grieved to hear about the death of Chief of Staff and his wife. I and Susan think and pray for their family, for families of other persons and for Indian Armed Forces. With deep respect and heavy heart we pray for early recovery of injured ones.

—Commander
US CENTCOM

✤✤✤

He is my friend; I respect his superb leadership in enhancing our distinctive strategic and global partnership. On behalf of JSDF, I express deep condolences on the death of CDS General Rawat, his wife and 11 other persons. May God grant peace to the souls of the deceased. Our heart goes to India.

—Director General of Intelligence Headquarters of Japan

✤✤✤

Sad news of sad demise of CDS Bipin Rawat and Madhulika Rawat has been a hard blow. We have lost a good friend, who had worked hard in furthering Indo-Maldives relations.

—Mariya Ahmed Didi
Defence Minister, Maldives

✤✤✤

"Deeply saddened by the tragic demise of CDS Gen Bipin Rawat, his wife, and several defence officials in a crash. My heartfelt condolences to the bereaved families and the Indian Armed Forces."

"We will remember CDS Rawat as a great military leader and a supporter of Flag of France-India defence ties," he said.

—Emmanuel Lenain
French envoy to India

✤✤✤

I had the fortune of meeting Rawat many times. His personality had courage of the highest order and deep love for the country. By shaking hands with him, heart and tongue would spontaneously say 'Jai Hind'.

—Anupam Kher
Noted Film Actor

✤✤✤

Bipin Rawat was a far-sighted person and a visionary

General Rawat was a far-sighted person and duty to the nation was paramount for him. His attempts in this direction would always be remembered. He was a deep thinker and promoter of Indian culture and had been motivating his colleagues with his own example of culture, ideology and dutifulness. They remember him in these words. Not only I had a glimpse of his exceptional, visionary and strong personality, but I learnt much from him. Today, General Rawat is not with us and a true tribute to him would be to try further the security programmes planned and initiated by him. A true tribute to him in perspective of Uttarakhand would be that people of Uttarakhand, wherever they are and whatever post they hold, work continuously with honesty and seriously for the progress of their state and its public.

Saying this Rana turns emotional, *"I and retired Col A.S. Bisht consider ourselves fortunate that we personally consigned ashes of these divine souls in five* prayags *(pilgrimage sites) of Devprayag, Rudraprayag, Karnaprayag, Nandprayag and Vishnuprayag." Time is a great healer. Today, amidst daily, physical and worldly responsibilities, General Rawat comes to our mind continuously. He is never forgotten, nor will he ever be." He said.*

—**Rear Admiral OPS Rana** (Retired)

✣✣✣

He was like a guardian for me

It is hard to believe that General Bipin Rawat is not with us. He was the pride of the country and state. In General Rawat's death, the country has suffered a great loss. The state of Uttarakhand has suffered the most. With his simplicity and clarity, it was difficult to believe that he was holding the top post of CDS. Brave martyr General Bipin Rawat had deep attachment with Uttarakhand. He was like a guardian for me. Even today, when I remember the time spent with him, my eyes brim with tears.

When General Rawat met me, he said, "I would take you to 'War Memorial', introduce you to soldiers' families; we would arrange 'bada khana' *in the evening." Then he said that four programmes would be organised in Uttarakhand—one in Kumaon Regiment, Ranikhet, second in Lansdowne, third in Dehradun and fourth in Banbasa Cantt. "In all the four places, we'll meet soldiers, soldiers' families and ex-servicemen."*

My last meeting with him took place on 9 November on the occasion of State Foundation Day. Both Madhulikaji and General had come. They had planned the programme on that day itself. Later, on 14 November, he called on Ganesh Joshiji's number and we had a long talk. Whenever he is mentioned, I become sentimental. I considered General Bipin Rawat as my guardian. General Rawat patronised and guided us in every way. One great thing about him was that he was such a lively person; whenever he was requested for any work, his reply would always be "Will be done". But destiny had some different decision for him.

—**Pushkar Singh Dhami,** Chief Minister, Uttarakhand

✤✤✤

Self-dependence in defence was his top priority

Country needs 'visionary leadership' in every field, whether it is politics, or defence security, ruling, administration or education. When India needed a firm military leadership, CDS General Bipin Rawat untimely left the world. This was the far-sightedness of CDS General Rawat that he speeded the efforts of making India self-dependent in the field of defence production. Among his priorities, first as Army Chief and then as CDS, self-dependence in defence field was on the top, whether it was in production of weapons or missile technology.

Besides the country, CDS Bipin Rawat had a deep desire of doing something for his home-state. He was greatly worried about the frontier areas of Uttarakhand. He usually discussed preserving the settlements in crucial frontier areas in view of outside danger to the security of the country, providing employment to the people of such areas, providing educational and health facilities. He shared these concerns with almost all of his near ones from time to time.

—**Trivendra Singh,** Former Chief Minister, Uttarakhand

Sainya Dham and their names

When I heard of his accident, I was attending a family function. 'Sunderkand' *was being recited. The moment I got the information, I started praying to God about the safety of General Sahib, but God had decided otherwise. May be He also needs good men and I visited his residence to offer condolences, then what I saw was unprecedented—perhaps people do not gather in such a large number even to honour important political leaders. Roads of Delhi were jammed; there were unending queues. Thereafter there was a stream of people the whole day.*

Once I asked General to give us a Recruitment Centre for the youth. The General replied, "Ganesh, I'll give you easily, you just do one thing. You ask me for a Centre for both, this place and another for Kumaon. 1,500 persons would get employment and our borders would also be secured." Such was the grand personality of General Rawat. Today, I am a minister, but when I met him, I was an MLA. His demeanor would disarm anyone. It was his way of showing respect that he never talked to me sitting on the chair of Chief. He would always come away to the Sofa and speak only once I used to sit. It was the year 2016-2017. I went to General Bipin Rawat during the period when I was MLA. I had one demand. Today, the youth of Uttarakhand are enjoying a relaxation of 5 cms. in their height for recruitment in the Army, which is because of General Bipin. I bow to him.

—**Ganesh Joshi,** Soldier Welfare Minister, Uttarakhand

✤✤✤

Such leaders are rarely seen in history

Sitting here on the bank of River Ganges, I am remembering this great son of devbhoomi, *who is now not among us. Such brave sons, such leaders, such patriots seldom and rarely appear in history. He was a warrior of different kind. I saw him in 1974 at National Defence Academy. Both of us were in the same squadron. I was one-and-a-half years senior. He was a source of great pride for our entire nation, for our Uttarakhand and our Pauri. His departure is as if all of us have lost someone of their own.*

The day might be in everyone's mind, when he was to be taken to Brar Square for last rites, how people were running ahead of him; how emotions were erupting. It was quite different. I had also lost a friend and squadron companion in General Rawat. Losing an NDA squadron mate is a personal loss to me. I worked with him as Brigade Commander in Kashmir. Both of us were Brigade Commanders and I saw him quite closely in challenging environments. There are many moments, many memories in my soldierly-life which are linked with him. Those were fortunate moments, when we got the opportunity to work with him.

Uttarakhand is the land of soldiers, land of valiant warriors. It is abode of soldiers and in which Bipin Rawat had added his historical chapter which is an inspiration for all of us.

—**Lt Gen** (retired) **Gurmeet Singh**
Governor, Uttarakhand

✤✤✤

During the 'Raibar' programme, CDS General Bipin Rawat and his wife Madhulika Rawat were given a lyrical tribute. Utttarakhand's eminent folk-singer, Rekha Uniyal Dhasmana presented a song specially written for General Rawat. She became emotional while singing the song and eyes of many among the audience were filled with tears

Song written for General Rawat:

रणबाँकुरों की भूमि च या
फिर आलो क्वी बिपिन रावत
रण सजालो बैरी भगालो
फिर आलो क्वी बिपिन रावत
आंखों मां छन हमरा आँसू
गाथा या गौरव की च
जय प्रहरी जय उत्तराखंड
मातृभूमि बिपिन रावत की च
उतराखंड मा जनम लीनी
उतराखंड को लाल च,
गर्व हमथैं तुम पर भारी
तुम हमारो सरताज च
सैंण गौं से निकली कि नेफा पहुँची
हिमालय की रक्षा करदू, बाटू-बाटू देखदि रै
त्वे जन फौजी, त्वे जना जनरल
मातृभूमि थें समर्पित रै
अंत बड़ो दुखदायी रै, अर जीवन साथी दगड़ा रै,
सात वचन, सात फेरा, साथ युग-युग कू निभै
अमर तेरी शान च, अर अमर तेरो नाम च
रण सजालो बैरी भगालो
फिर आलो क्वी बिपिन रावत
जय उतराखंड, जजय देवभूमि
जय सैंण गौं, जय उतराखंड
जय हिंद, जय हिंद, जय हिंद, जय हिंद!

—Rekha Uniyal Dhasmana
Lyricist

I'll remain indebted to him forever

I had been associated with General Bipin Rawat for almost 10 years. I came in his contact, when he was Major General in Eastern Command, Calcutta. I consider myself fortunate and proud. He always took care of me. Whenever there was a problem, I would seek his guidance. I tried to follow his guidance completely. I have been with ITBP, CRPF, working as Additional DG Operations during the last two years. Whenever I faced a problem, I would contact General Rawat unhesitatingly.

Most of the deployment of ITBP is in the remote hills of Uttarakhand. Whether it is Harsil or Niti-Mana or Vyas Valley, all these areas are uninhabited. It is very difficult to provide complete security to these areas. We have been deployed on the Chinese and Nepal borders and we try to implement all relevant government schemes. Being the native of Uttarakhand, I always try to participate in all the programmes the government has launched. I'll always be indebted to him for providing guidance in discharging my duties.

—**Manoj Rawat,** ADG, ITBP

❖❖❖

His advice on border management will always be remembered

My interaction with him was just a year old before his untimely death. When I got familiarised with him, we had requested him that Uttarakhand Police would be benefitted from his experience and for this we invited him to Police Headquarters. He accepted our invitation gracefully. We discussed border management with him. We met him during the 'State Foundation Day' organised by the Governor. Who knew that the time would snatch him from us so early?

He promised to come and further discuss about Uttarakhand. While discussing border management with him, certain issues emerged. He gave some important suggestions. Our international border is adjacent to both China and Nepal. Problems of both the borders are different. We discussed matters with the CDS for about one hour.

—**Ashok Kumar,** DGP, Uttarakhand Police

❖❖❖

Salute to the pinnacle man of proud Uttarakhand traditions

His departure is an irreparable loss. General Bipin Rawat was a great Army Chief, and more than that, he was a humble person too. He never differentiated between people based on their rank or position. He was equally related to everyone. It has always been an experience meeting him that we Uttarakhandis feel proud of. General Bipin Rawat had been a pinnacle man of that proud tradition of Uttarakhand that has been inspiring the sons of the devbhoomi *to serve the motherland. His military career of four decades is a proof of this, for which he placed his family second to the nation. That was his dedication to the country, which we witnessed in the sea of humanity stunned at his departure, during his last journey.*

I and Bholeji had been fortunate enough to meet him several times. He had a different kind of energy within. He wanted to do a lot after fulfilling his military responsibilities. Whenever we met him, he used to express his concern for Uttarakhand. He would convey what could be done for Uttarakhand; what role the Army is playing in border and remote areas of Uttarakhand. His vision for Uttarakhand was different from others. He used to talk about horticulture in hilly areas and about medical facilities in those areas. He would express his concern as to how the children could get education. He would talk about steely resolve of the women of this place.

I listened to his younger daughter, who was telling that her father was trying to learn Garhwali words. He was noting brief notes in his diary, which indicate that he was preparing himself for the service of devbhoomi. *We often heard him talk of what is good for the hills, what could jointly be done for hills.*

—Matashree Mangalaji
Founder and Patron, Hans Foundation

✣✣✣

Very few persons were aware of my mother's contribution

My father was a Gorkha soldier and an infantry man from heart. His heart, mind and everything else were dedicated to the nation. As a General, all know about my father and his contribution, but contribution of our mother is known to only a few ones. In all the programmes, we are known as daughters of Madhu and this was our identity. My father, CDS Bipin Rawat was, however, considered a highly dedicated officer for his military services. He had been posted for a very long period at different remote places on the borders of the country. He had been busy in important responsibilities and used to be out of house. Mother single-handedly excellently nurtured both the daughters, though in later years, my father would get some time and the family to a large extent could live together. But, I would like to say that my mother's contribution too was important and must be remembered.

—Kritika
Elder daughter of CDS Bipin Rawat

✣✣✣

My father was trying to learn Garhwali. One day, I went to his table near his bed, where I saw a pad which had handwritten notes. Out of curiosity, I saw that booklet-type notepad and I found that Father had scribbled some Garhwali words along with their meanings and details. He was trying to learn Garhwali. It was heartening to note that he was so serious about learning his native dialect that he was preparing regular notes.

—Tarini
Younger daughter of CDS Bipin Rawat

□□□

General Bipin Rawat : A Profile

Name : Bipin Rawat

Birth : 16 March, 1958, Dehradun (Uttarakhand)

Demise : 8 December, 2021

Father : Lt Gen Lakshman Singh Rawat

Mother : Sushila Rawat

Wife : Madhulika Rawat

Daughters : Kratika and Tarini

Education : MG Academy; Cambrian Hall School, Dehradun; and Saint Edward School, Shimla.

College/Military Academy : National Defence Academy (BSc); Defence Services Staff College (DSSC), Wellington; Indian Military Academy (IMA); United States Army Command and General Staff College; Chaudhary Charan Singh University, Meerut (PhD).

Army Career Rank : 2nd Lieutenant 16 December, 1978; Lieutenant 16 December, 1980; Captain 31 July, 1984: Major 16 December, 1989; Lt Col 1 June, 1998; Colonel 1 August, 2003; Brigadier 1 October, 2007; Major General 20 October, 2011; Lieutenant General 1 June, 2014; General (Army Chief) 1 January, 2017; General (Chief of the Army Staff) 30 December, 2019.

Appointments : Chief of Defence Staff 1 January, 2020-8 December, 2021; 57th Chairman, Chiefs of Staff Committee 27 September, 2019-31 December, 2019; 26th Army Chief 31 December, 2016-31 December, 2019; 37th Vice Chief of the Army 1 September, 2016-31 December, 2016.

Awards : Padma Vibhushan (posthumously), Param Vishisht Seva Medal, Uttam Yudh Seva Medal, Ati Vishisht Seva Medal, Yudh Seva Medal, Army Medal, Vishisht Seva Medal.